Make me an Offer

and

A Kid for Two Farthings

Make me an Offer

and

A Kid for Two Farthings

by
Wolf Mankowitz

Illustrated by
Leonard Rosoman & James Boswell

ANDRE DEUTSCH

74220l

This book was first published in 1955 under a joint
Reader's Union/André Deutsch imprint

This new edition published in 1990
by André Deutsch Limited
105-106 Great Russell Street London WC1B 3LJ

British Library cataloguing in Publication Data

Mankowitz, Wolf, *1924-*
    Make me an offer; A kid for two farthings.
    I. Title
    823'.914 [F]

ISBN 0 233 98548 4

Make Me An Offer first published by
André Deutsch Limited July 1952
Second impression August 1952
Third impression 1954

A Kid For Two Farthings first published by
André Deutsch Limited September 1953
Second impression November 1953
Third impression 1955

Printed and bound in Great Britain by
WBC Limited, Bristol and Maesteg

Make me an Offer ✦ ✦ ✦ ✦ ✦ ✦

Illustrated by Leonard Rosoman ✦ ✦ ✦ ✦ ✦ ✦

Peleus, Thetis, Aphrodite?

ONE

As far as I know it started when I was about eleven.

One Sunday my mother made some sandwiches for us and my father took me to the British Museum by tram. We got shilling all-day tickets, which meant we could go anywhere in the world so long as we went by tram. So that we went a very long way round to the Museum and as soon as we got there we ate the sandwiches sitting on the bench by the Easter Island statue. They were chicken sandwiches and we couldn't look at anything until we had eaten them. Then we went to the Egyptian Room which was my father's favourite and he showed me the man in the stone tomb. He was crumpled up with his skin stretched very tight and the colour of kippers. To tell you the truth, he made my mouth water because at that time I was always hungry.

We looked at the Assyrian bulls and some Phoenician glass and quite soon I saw the Vase. Afterwards I went to the Museum often and I found a lot of things there, but I always went to the Vase first. I always went to see it again before I left. I used to watch it carefully waiting for it to move, and once it did very slightly. I had my own way of looking at the Vase. First I looked at one side for a while; then the other side; then I walked round it from left to right; then I walked round it from right to left.

Once or twice in bed at night I worried about whether it was quite safe. Maybe someone was waiting until the doors were closed to steal it. I gritted my teeth to think of it lying in pieces on the floor. Once I opened the window of my room and looked out over the small back gardens. It was a warm summer night and I could smell the stocks my mother planted. The air was deep blue and very solid, and I thought suddenly that the Vase was solid night carved with figures of pure light. Then I became interested in chemistry and made a bench to work on in my room. I filled the room with chlorine once and another time I blew my eyebrows off in the lavatory and my mother gave me a Steedman's shock powder. The last time I saw the Vase I had a plan worked out for stealing it and I hung about for a whole day almost. Then I left the Vase for half an hour to have a look at the Prehistoric Room and it was suddenly closing time and my plan had gone wrong because there was a guard standing right behind me.

I didn't ever completely forget about the Vase though. I wrote a prize essay in the School Christmas Contest about it. *In 1594 in a sepulchral chamber beneath the Monte del Grano a small hill near Rome, the ashes of Alexander*

Severus and those of his mother were discovered. What happened to the ashes no one can say, but the urn containing them passed first to the museum of the Capitol, thence to the Palace of the Barbarini. In 1770 a Scottish antiquary in Rome, one James Byres by name, acquired the urn. In 1782 Sir William Hamilton, Ambassador to the Court of Naples, bought it for £1,000. The Duchess of Portland bought it from him secretly, and after her death the Duke of Portland purchased it at a sale of the late Duchess's private museum in Whitehall. In this way the urn containing the ashes of the Emperor Alexander Severus and his mother became the Portland Vase. . . .

My father kept the essay, but soon after a boy at school whose fingers and clothes were always stained yellow with picric acid introduced me to the study of alkaloids. We kept nearly twenty different alkaloids in old tins, and he distilled a new one from violets which he called Violene. We wrote a paper about it and I bought a large glass flask to put it in. I don't believe I thought again of the Vase until years afterwards when my father brought home a black and white Wedgwood copy of it. It was a modern copy and not very good. I was buying at the auctions for my father at that time, and he asked me to find out when the first Wedgwood copies were made. I went to the British Museum to find out and as soon as I got there I went to see the Vase. I walked round it once or twice, then I went to the ceramics department and asked to see the Wedgwood copy. They stood over me while I looked at it. They moved a little closer to me when I touched it, and when I picked it up the curator gave a little scream and his short beard jogged up and down.

I went home and told my father that his Portland was no good, like his Constable painting and his Nuremberg cup, and for the first time in years I thought about the Vase. The glass one which had held the ashes was an urn all right. It was wonderful but in the end it was only complete if the

9

ashes of a dead man and his mother were in it. But the Portland a potter named J. Wedgwood made in 1789, that was a vase – a real vase, perfect and complete and alone. And after that I always looked at Portland Vases to find a first one.

I suppose all this must have had something to do with my becoming a dealer in English pottery, but I can find all kinds of other reasons. What does it matter anyway? I never found a first Portland. I collected all the books relating to Wedgwood, and many magazines and news cuttings. I carried one cutting about with me in my wallet until the folds rubbed through. It was a piece from the *Morning Chronicle* of 1886. 'Stolen from the collection of Mr Daniel Drage. Three salt-glaze pew groups valued at £650, a pair of 15 inch Whieldon tortoise-shell glaze standing figures valued at £300, and an old Wedgwood green copy of the Portland Vase. The Curator of the Wedgwood Museum at Etruria tells us that there is no known record of the great Josiah having made a green Portland copy. The police are investigating the crime and doubtless the thief will be detected when these famous and rare items of English pottery are offered for sale. Mr Drage's collection, an expert writes, is worth in the neighbourhood of £40,000 and is one of the finest in the world. Mr Drage was on the Continent at the time of the burglary, in which entrance was effected from the garden behind the house.'

Once or twice that green Portland gave me a bad time; or it could have done if I had believed in it. And yet Old Drage knew the stuff well. Dealers still like to say they have something from his collection. And yet no matter how well you know the game, you can be wrong. But I liked to carry the cutting around with me as a sort of magic charm. If Josiah had ever made a solid green jasper Portland I wanted to see it before the close of business.

I met a man once in the tea-room on Liverpool Street Station. He was a short, thin man with a marked curvature of the spine which made him look as if he had a bad pain, and when he swallowed his tea he wrinkled his face up as if it tasted like epsom salts. I said to him the tea was too strong, and he told me how the tannin coated your stomach and turned the delicate membranes into leather. 'I should only drink milk,' he said. 'Milk is soothing to the delicate membranes. It nutrifies the stomach without straining it. You got to soothe the membranes,' he told me.

I told him I liked milk and he stopped fighting me. We had another cup of tea and soothed the membranes for a while longer. He was a button manufacturer and in twenty years he had sold more than seventeen million buttons. 'Put side by side maybe they would circle the world,' he said. 'Who has the time to do it?' I asked him, and he agreed sadly that it wasn't worth while. 'But,' he said, 'don't misunderstand me. There is a great future for buttons.' He pulled me closer to him, and dipped his hand into his waistcoat pocket. Then he showed me the only solid gold button with a two carat diamond in it in the world.

I was like that man. I wanted to believe there was a future in pots, and I thought of that future as a green Portland. I was looking hard, and finding a fair living, but pretty soon I would have to start drinking milk five times a day to soothe the delicate membranes.

TWO

THAT evening we had just stopped wrestling with the right way to bring up children, and given the baby a bottle. He liked it all right, and even let go of the teat for a moment to laugh. His soft yellow hair was flat across his great forehead, plastered down with tears. But his smile was full of satisfaction and triumph. He'd pulled it off once again, and was getting to feel infallible. I knew how he felt. I felt the same way when I managed to run something at the auctions—run it so high it was no use any more to whoever bought it. We laughed back at the baby, but he was busy now dragging on the teat. He had his hands gently placed on the sides of the bottle, and his eyes were already glazed with satisfaction.

Whilst we were there we had a look at the other boy.

He was curled up with his knees almost touching his stomach. The bed-clothes were kicked away and his pyjama trousers had slipped down over his backside. We covered him up and he murmured 'Black man' and turned over. Black man was his favourite game at the moment. He liked to play it on his own for an hour or so every morning, wearing nothing but the belt from his blue dressing gown weaved around his waist and loins.

My wife said, 'He's breathing through his mouth again.'

'How else should he breathe?'

'I'll give him some drops tomorrow.'

'So long as he breathes,' I said. 'Let's eat now.' The baby still had his eyes open but he'd stopped drawing on the bottle. He hadn't needed it. It was just that he liked to feel he could have it. I certainly knew how that baby felt about life. It was a wonderful feeling, and it didn't happen very often. For my part he could have a whole bar next to his cot and just take a nip whenever he fancied it.

I hadn't eaten much that day. I had to get out early to catch a dealer in Baker Street before he went out buying. He was the brother-in-law of a man who had some tri-coloured jasper cameos I needed. The man had decided not to sell to me. He was rich and temperamental and it hurt him in the heart whenever he thought someone might be making a profit on him. But the brother-in-law was poor and the rich man made a charity – his only charity – out of letting him take things on approval from time to time. The brother-in-law would get them for me, but I had to get to his basement shop before he started out on his rounds. I drank two cups of China tea without milk or sugar, kissed the family all round, fixed the boy's conductor's hat so that he could see me to the gate, and went off.

Lunch had got lost somehow between an auction at Phillips, Son & Neale in Blenheim Street, and an appointment with a big American dealer back at the Shop. I got what I wanted at Phillips'. I bought a yellow and white jasper Portland Vase and a pair of basaltes vases. I gave Mrs Toshak, the interior decorator, three pounds on the vases for not bidding against me, and I got back to the shop just before the American arrived. He turned out to be a soft-spoken Baghdadi with a big pasty-faced American in tow as bookkeeper.

'I can spend fifty or five-hundred pounds,' he said with a sad smile. 'Don't let us argue over price – name it and I will say yes or no. Is that all right?'

'Have the five hundred ready,' I said, 'I wouldn't insult you by taking less.'

In the finish it wasn't quite up to scratch. But it was four hundred we needed – who doesn't need four hundred? – and I went home satisfied. My wife was vaguely surprised to hear that grown men could spend so much time and subtlety and money on vases, but she was impressed by the degree of the folly. And I was just about ready to put myself round the lamb stew she had in the oven when the baby started growling. Then when that was all settled and my stomach was beginning to sob for a little sustenance the telephone rang.

I said to my wife, 'Don't put it back in the oven – I don't want to lose any time when I get back,' and went out to the phone. I picked it up and a voice blared at me.

'You don't want your coal.'

'No,' I said.

'We've run out of coal,' the voice blared on.

'Have my coal, Mr Sparta,' I said.

'Good boy, Charlie,' the bear answered. 'You'll order it tomorrow.'

'That's it,' I said. And then it came to me like all the best ideas, out of the middle of nothing, into the middle of nothing. 'I wanted to see you about something, Mr Sparta,' I said.

'You know where I am,' the bear grunted, 'so come up and see me.' I went back to the kitchen with a smile on my face.

'Put it in the oven, angel. I've got some business to do with Sparta.'

'Charlie,' she called as I opened the door, 'ask him if I can keep the big pram in his toolshed.'

I don't know where Abe Sparta found his name but he certainly was a self-made Greek. Maybe it was the poet in him which made him pick out Sparta for a name instead of Lwow – maybe he had a classical education. Whatever it was that made him my landlord I respected it. It isn't every Odessa lumberman who can stay out of prison long enough to become a respectable dealer in timber. Abe was a clever man all right. I had the lower part of the house which was damp, and he was upstairs, away from it all, and safer from burglars. It gave the old man palpitations every time he used those stairs, but it was certainly safer from burglars. He had a long-standing affection for large items in silver-gilt – Victorian pieces, angels with and without cherubs, *putti*, festoons, devices, motifs, fruit, flowers and dead game. Impressive stuff worth about four shillings an ounce – but to him, civilisation hall-marked with elegance. Back home a family with a pair of thin silver candlesticks was respectable. Sparta was just a homely boy at heart.

He was a big, broad, curving old man with a heavy moustache and down-turned eyes tucked away among grizzled eyebrows. He spoke a rich cockney flavoured with Yiddish phrases and gestures, and though he was well into the seventies now he still couldn't resist a little business. I think the only reason why he bought this old Regency house was that he had nothing to do one day and was just poking around doing it when he saw the place was up for sale. He walked around tugging at this and that. There were little terraces and porches all over the house then and it settled him when he found they were made of lead. Lead was fetching £117 a ton. I think he cleared his purchase money on the lead, and though the place looked a little bald, stripped of it all, it still had a certain quality about it.

It was on a hill in a hundred yards of old houses which hadn't been developed yet, and the whole place had an atmosphere which made up for the damp. I'd like to think well of Sparta's feeling for beauty – but it was the lead all right. It's amazing how little lead makes a ton. I had tried to talk to Sparta about other things, the weather and the garden and life but he only rose to business. If you said to him: 'That was a nice little deal today,' or 'Heard about a good sale next week?' some sort of animation would crease up his forehead and bring a little lustre to his eyes. I was looking forward to seeing that lovelight now.

The position was this. A man I know in Chelsea buys gilded frames. He burns the frames and collects the gold and somehow it shows him a living. Now, when he's looking for frames he sees other things – bits of china, carved mantelpieces, and so on, and so he's in a position to put you on to a good thing now and then, if dropping the odd fiver doesn't give you gallstones. I'm no philanthropist but I believe in friendship, and in this case my belief in human nature has been justified on several occasions. I nearly got a pair of Chelsea birds through him once. I was young at the time and I took an older dealer along with me – an expert he was – to have a look at a load of china an old woman had cleared out of the attic. It was junk all right. I could see that and was counting the pieces to reckon them at a bob apiece all round. Then I dug out these birds – raised anchor mark, right as rain, just a little chipping on the leaves.

'What have you there?' screams this experienced lunatic.

'Just a couple of old birds,' I said. The old woman had looked up with a slight gleam in her eyes.

'You fool,' he said to me – he was calling me a fool. Then he turned to the old lady who looked as though she had just conceived, so brilliant was the light in her eyes. 'Madam,' he said, 'these birds are Chelsea and very valuable. I will give you two hundred pounds for them.'

I wanted him to drop dead more than I have ever wanted anything.

'Gord,' the old woman said. 'If you'd have said fifty bob you could have had 'em. I'll send them up to London to my nephew who works in a solicitor's office. They must be worth a fortune.'

He looked at me with the wide-open eyes of a moron. It suited him perfectly. I left him there still looking. Maybe he's still there. It breaks my heart to think of those birds.

I had only just got into the shop the other morning when this friend rings me. I was reading the fifth letter that month from an old gentleman who had an original copy of the Portland Vase. It had been in his family for years, and he didn't really want to sell it unless he got a very good offer. I could just see the slightly insane smile of subtlety on the face of the provincial dealer who wrote that letter. I wrote a polite note offering him a fiver just for fun, and then the phone rang. I let it ring for a while to show my independence, and then picked it up.

'You still after Wedgwood?'

'Yes.'

'Well, come over and see me.'

'Who are you?'

'Fred here, you know. Frames.'

'Yes, Fred. What have you got?'

'Nothing. But I know where it is.'

'All right, I'll be over.'

I saw him later that morning. His shop was in a mews, and he was fitted in neatly at the back between two high stacks of frames. I crawled over to him and he told me all about it without wasting his valuable time on vulgar pleasantries.

'This place here is a break-up job – period house – hundred rooms – Sir someone-or-other, Christ knows. Whole room plastered in Wedgwood, big, small, everything, all Wedgwood. You want it?'

I made it clear that I wanted it. I said, 'Maybe.'

'No one knows about it – got the catalogue up in the country.'

'Let's have a look,' I said, without enthusiasm.

The catalogue was one of those amateurish plush jobs a small country auctioneer gets the local printer to dream up when he accidently get his hands on something good. They even spelt Wedgwood wrong. But it was certainly a lot of Wedgewood. I gave him a couple of pounds on account and went off with the catalogue in my pocket.

When I got back to the shop my manager was selling a Civil Servant a pot in black and white jasper. 'In fine sunlight,' she sang, 'these colours will look delightful – black and white jasper is something we often send out to India – it's so civilised looking amongst all that Oriental stuff.' The Civil Servant remembered he was civilised and took it. She came bounding up to the office five minutes later. I let her tell me all about it so as not to deprive her of one of the few real satisfactions in a dealer's life. 'So I said to him, "it looks wonderful in bright sunlight",' she went on.

'Did you ever see it in bright sunlight?' I interrupted, and threw her the catalogue.

'Can't they even spell Wedgwood right?' she asked.

'How do you reckon it?' I asked.

'How can you say,' she answered, 'who'll be there?'

That was the whole point. That was why I was letting my dinner get dried up now. That was why I was going to talk on an empty stomach.

I went up to Abe Sparta's flat. The door was open and I could hear him hawking in the sitting-room. His wife was drying the dishes in the kitchen. She dropped one as I knocked on his door.

'Break up the rest,' he shouted. 'What good are they? Come in Charlie. The plates she breaks. Have you got any plates in your shop? Bring them along. She'll break 'em. Sit down.'

'That's a nice big fire,' I said.

'Don't forget the coal. You want a cigar?' He knew I never smoked a cigar so I didn't put his back up by taking one now.

'Sit down,' he grunted, hunching closer to the fire.

'I got something good today,' I said, lighting a cigarette.

'So that's all right about the coal then – I can rely on you.'

I was taking it too fast. It was only manners to talk about the coal for a while. 'You burn a lot of coal,' I said with admiration in my voice.

'More than a hundredweight and a half a week,' Sparta said with pride, looking up at me with a challenge in his eyes asking me to call him a liar. 'Nearly two hundredweight,' he rasped, spitting into the fire.

'It's a lot of coal,' I suggested.

Honour was satisfied now, so he leaned back and said in what passed with him for a friendly tone, 'Nu, Charlie boy – what's the excitement.'

I gave him the catalogue, and he spent the next two minutes skimming over it. Then he gave it back to me.

'The break-up boys will be there.'

'Yes,' I agreed.

'So this panelling will fetch its price.'

'I don't reckon the panelling.'

'So what else is there to reckon?'

'I'll pay two and a half for the Wedgwood.'

He made a swallowing movement and moved his lips silently. 'That's about as much as the panelling's worth. What will you do with the panelling?'

'Sell it to you,' I said.

'How are you going up?' he replied.

'By train.'

'Find out the trains, Charlie. I'll come with you.'

As I ate my dinner I worked it out the way Sparta saw it. If I said two hundred and fifty for the Wedgwood, he reckoned three hundred and fifty. If he said two hundred and fifty for the panelling it was worth twice that. Maybe it sounds complicated to you but sparing the technical details it means we could both see a profit in the deal.

My wife was ironing a new shirt of mine.

'Take the bones out, honey,' I suggested.

'It's your dinner – you take them out,' she said.

'Out of the shirt collar I mean.'

'Did you ask him about the big pram in his toolshed?' she answered.

'No,' I said.

'I don't know what you put bones in the collar for, anyway,' she grumbled, fiddling with the shirt.

'In my trade you have to look smart,' I said.

THREE

THAT night I dreamt my father sold the lease of my shop and bought a two and a half year lease on a shop in Jermyn Street. He paid £2,600 for it and the rent was £465 inclusive. I came back from the country and a new shop front was already installed. There was no room for anything except jewellery. I hate dealing in jewellery.

'The rent's cheaper,' he kept saying.

'Who cares about the rent,' I screamed. 'I need a place I can turn round in – I'm a big boy now.'

It doesn't sound like a nightmare, but I woke up with sweat on my forehead. The bedclothes were over my face and for a while I kept on looking into the window of that little shop and screaming. Then I reached out and put my hand on my wife's thigh. It was warm and I wanted to go to sleep again with my hand there, but she jerked away suddenly, as if I was a roadsweeper trying to feel the brush texture in one of the paintings at Wildenstein's. For two seconds I could have cried. There's nothing so lonely as the middle of the night with the floorboards creaking and the feeling about you that you're out of business. I reached up to switch the light on, but the lights in that shop had been on and the dark was more restful.

I was alone all right, just as she was alone in the middle of whatever business kept her asleep. The baby was working out his next deal. The boy was alone scheming out the next move in Black Man. Maybe only Abe Sparta was awake like me.

The floorboards somewhere creaked for what seemed like an hour. Maybe he was lifting his legs out of bed. They would feel like lead – cold and dead – but not worth £117 a ton. In his sitting room the fire would be out and the warmth in the air worn off. I reached out and felt round for the flask of water on the bedside table. I drew it over and felt for the mouth with my lips. But the water had a dusty, stale feel to it.

I got up to make tea – I poured the tea into a glass and squeezed some lemon into it. When you walk around in the middle of the night it takes a while before you can really say you're thinking about anything particular. Your eyes look downwards and if there's a paper on the table you follow the words out meaninglessly. It was the paper of the day before yesterday. A story on page three told how an important contractor was in trouble over an army surplus sale which had been knocked out. Someone said it was tantamount to robbing the country. 'It is a practice which is as much criminal as unpatriotic.' About as criminal as the income tax collector assessing you for next year on the profits he thought you made the year before last.

The knock-out is not something I have much to do with. I don't have to mix with such people. I am a specialist. This means I have so little money that I can only deal in one thing – but it also means that in that line I can buy and sell higher than anyone else. My father taught me to specialise.

About twenty years ago my father was a market-man. He had a stall with shutters in a semi-enclosed market in East London. The rent was twenty-six shillings a week and he was down as a general dealer because he didn't know what he was going to sell. There were two reasons for this. One was he didn't know anything about selling. The other was he didn't have any money. He used to borrow five pounds from a man called Segal on Monday, and on Saturday night he used to pay him back seven pounds. Now the whole of my father's economic life was constructed on the principle of meeting Segal. He tried buying cheap cutlery in the Houndsditch and found he couldn't meet Segal. He bought fancy goods and found he owed Segal more money than he had stock. He tried some attractive boxes of handkerchiefs and ties and bowler hats. But Segal was disappointed in him. Then he became a specialist.

For ten shillings a lot he bought ten lots of odd army boots. He brought them back from the sale room and filled up the shop with them. My mother went home in tears to fry roe for dinner. Then he stood in the middle of all those odd boots and started sorting them into pairs. Then he covered the whole stall with pairs sorted into sizes and started to sell them at two-an-sixpence a pair. That week he met Segal and hurt his feelings by not taking a fiver for next week. He was a specialist and out of the clutch of common usurers.

What a week-end that was! He bought my mother the

largest box of liqueur chocolates she had ever seen. He bought us all presents and he was laughing all the time. He sat at the table after dinner with his tea getting cold in front of him, and put his head in his hands and laughed till he was shaking all over. His hands had the black from the boots ingrained in them and they looked terribly strong. After that he always specialised. It was something different every week, but whatever it was the place was full of it. And always it was something the poor wanted and always it was cheaper than it had ever been before. One week it was blacking for grates – then it was perfume and we were spraying all the old women with it – then it was women's hats and we all wore them. Once it was iron tonic and my father stood in his shirt sleeves showing his muscles and joking with the women while they bought it. Once it was a cellar of old claret bought at threepence a bottle. Everyone was tasting it and buying it instead of invalid port. It was just as good. And all the detective force came round to tell us we needed a licence to sell it and to buy a few crates.

When I started in business on Saturday afternoons selling foreign stamps on a corner of the stall, I already knew how to specialise. I used to buy Foreign and Colonial mixture in small sacks at a place in London Wall and put it into small packets at a penny and threepence. My father financed me to begin with, but it never worried me to meet him on Saturday nights. We used to have a cup of tea and a cheese cake at teatime at the coffee-stall in the corner of the market, and discuss business prospects. 'You should always specialise,' he would say. 'We're specialists,' I used to answer. 'What else?' he would say, and start to laugh.

I was thinking about my father and wondering why I should dream he was a bad business man. Between sipping my tea I drummed on the table with my fingers and hummed a tune quietly.

What is it that makes you eat
Bananas and cat's meat?

It was a little thing my father had composed and which he used to sing when he was worried. He pronounced 'eat' as 'it' and 'it' as 'eat' – so it rhymed. He also made three words of 'bananas' – so it scanned. I never read anything which had the poignant truth of that poem.

It worried me especially that I should be worried just now when things were going so well. My speciality had moved from foreign stamps to Wedgwood. I was once asked to chair a ring. It was like the top of a short ladder.

Here I was getting ready to go for a trip into the country to try to buy a whole room in the sort of house you pay half-a-crown to be shown round on a wet Saturday afternoon. With Abe Sparta I might even buy it. And I was worried. It was never having anything to do with the knock-out that worried me. I was used to going to the auctions for my one or two lots and either buying them or making them so expensive they weren't profitable any more to whoever bought them against me. After a while the trade got used to seeing me around whenever there was Wedgwood selling. They left me alone on the whole, or just ran a little way to show spirit and left the bidding before it cost them too much. In bidding you have to have a sense of how far the other man is going to go. It isn't as difficult as it sounds. You can be fairly certain that if you bid twenty-eight, the man behind you will go thirty. But if you bid thirty he'll think twice and let you have it. You have to watch the tens – most people think in decimals.

It's a funny game, this dealing. Nothing's worth anything until you sell it, and then it's worth whatever you can get for it. You can't get anything at all unless you have the goods, so you have to buy them whether you know you can sell them or not. Everyone reckons goods differently – some dealers can't leave bronzes alone, or ormulu. There's an old short man with a great face like a pasty baby, and thick glasses pressed into his bulbous nose who can't leave bird's eye maple alone. When he sees bird's eye maple a sort of lust grips him. His hands tremble and his eyes turn inwards as if he had some little shrine there on which bird's eye maple was the only permitted sacrifice. He bids on and on and he gets it. He used to manufacture bedroom suites and now he pays the price by having to buy them all back. It's like those souls in hell you read about who have to go on doing just what they did in life. I've often watched him shaking away there as if he was praying. You don't know whether to laugh or be sick. Everyone runs him. The auctioneer trots him like a high-stepping racehorse pacing an old grey work donkey. And when he's finished he wipes beads of sweat off his forehead with his shaking fist all knotted up like a baby rubbing his eyes.

But all buying is like that. You get the bit between your teeth sometimes. Your heart pounds away like the first time you made love to a woman and you were frightened and couldn't do it properly. You suddenly have to have a big Sèvres vase or a collection of netsukes. And afterwards you feel as if you had passed a test – only it wasn't an intelligence test. Or you've come through the onset of a dangerous fever. Then you look at the figures you've scribbled in the catalogue and see just how much weight you've lost.

More often though, there's no feeling in it. The Sèvres vase is worth just so much to whoever buys it. Everyone wants it. And that's where the knock-out comes into being, born out of the ingenuity dealers have always given to the problems of survival. Seven dealers want it – one buys it. The seven meet and auction it again between themselves. Whoever gets it puts the extra money into the kitty and it's split seven ways. He can still make a profit on it, and everyone else makes their expenses. Who's to make laws for how a man should make a living? Life makes him a dealer and then he has to deal. Dealing's all anarchy – everyone's his own boss, he spends his own money, and goes bankrupt in his own way. Dealing is buying and selling – sometimes buying cheap and selling dear – sometimes buying dear and selling cheap. Everyone's after the dealer to make him pay a little more for what he's buying. Everyone wants to buy from him a little cheaper than he's selling. He's made money a hundred times, but he's lost it sixty. If you want to be unpleasant about it, dealing is sordid, and the dealer is a whore. But you won't pretend that whoring isn't hard work or that it doesn't supply a need. We don't have to be in love with the customer. We just have to take him upstairs. Anything after that is a cultural question. I'm no better, nor fundamentally different from the girl trading on Birdcage Walk on a wet Saturday evening. When things are bad my standards and my prices go down. But I want to do a better class of business if I can. Everything depends on it. First we look for a way of making a living, an existence. Then we find we have a standard of living. Then we learn about better standards, always further and further away from a woman crying into the frying oil on a Friday night. Are you trying to tell me that all this isn't progress? If you don't like dealing, try to do without it. You'll manage all right. But leave dealers and people who like to deal with them, leave auctioneers and knock-out men and profits and losses alone. It's a philosophy. You can have a different philosophy if you like but you can't alter this one.

So I agree with the knock-out but I don't work it. But here I was on to something new, and a knock-out might be the only way. I was reckoning on someone being there for that room, and I wanted to buy it when it was knocked-out. I wanted to sell the timber panelling straight away to Abe

27

and clear the Wedgwood plaques as a profit. And already it seemed to me I was being too clever. It worried me to be too clever. It felt like I was asking for something to trip me up. Supposing I took the room after the knock-out and Abe wouldn't take the timber. I would have to sell it to someone else quickly. I didn't know how to price it – I didn't know how to sell it. And I didn't have the money to play with, anyway.

It all came to that in the end: I didn't have the money. And this Wedgwood room was something for a Wedgwood specialist to get a touch of fever about. Already I was thinking about how much profit it would make and how long it would take to clear it and how I would offer the plaques. A little more thinking and the detail about not having the money wouldn't stop me. I could feel it coming on. I had to have it.

I drank all the tea in the pot. I felt tired with working it out this way and that. When I thought of coming back from the country with a few pounds in my pocket over my expenses and not a piece of Wedgwood to show, a feeling of faint sickness came into my stomach. My head felt empty now and I was hungry. I cut some bread and cheese and made a sandwich. I read a copy of Joe Miller's Jest Book while I ate. I had bought it that day from a runner for twenty-five shillings. The covers were missing and it was bound in a piece of brown paper. I found three jokes I had heard at the Palladium a couple of weeks back. They still made me laugh, and after I'd eaten another sandwich, I thought I felt better and went back to bed.

I got under the blankets quietly but my wife sighed and turned round. 'What's the matter?' she croaked.

'I was hungry,' I said.

'What's the time then?' she said. It was four o'clock.

'Nearly tomorrow already,' she said faintly.

'I might go out to the country tomorrow,' I said as if to

make conversation. 'I said I might go out to a sale for a couple of days.'

But she was asleep again. Women don't worry like we do.

FOUR

I LEFT early the next morning, just as soon as I could get
through reading Dan Dare to the boy. My wife still acted
a little as if she was asleep and talked about having a
woman to tea with a little boy from up the road who was
always hitting his baby sister. The baby was in his high-
chair carefully putting a spoonful of tomato pulp into his
right ear. His eyes were alight with discovery when I
kissed him goodbye on the top of his head just above where
it hadn't quite closed up yet. I could feel his pulse with my
lips. The boy escorted me to the garage and backed me out

like a policeman. He told me to wait a minute and put a policeman's hat on to do the job better.

I switched the lights on in the shop, glanced through the post, locked the door and drew some cash out of the safe. Then I left a note for my manager, looked up the route, locked the shop and went back to the car. The telephone was ringing when I left and I thought there goes my big chance of buying something really good.

I hate driving. I never can believe that I really control the machine under my hands. Why doesn't it rush up on to the pavement and do a little window shopping? Why doesn't it throw me into the nearest lamp-post? But I couldn't waste the day by travelling down by train just to view. If I went by road I could make a few calls and perhaps buy something here and there. I was going partly to show myself that it wasn't so important after all. I wanted to get over to it and take a quick look and tell myself it was Victorian and forget it. Then I could tell Abe Sparta it wasn't worth thinking about, and I wouldn't have to bother about finding the few hundreds my enthusiasm might cost me. That's what I wanted, but there was no point in losing opportunities. I might as well buy anything worth buying while I was out.

I was taking the car out of Regent's Park by the Hanover Gate, and noticing as I always did when I passed that way that there was a pair of overlay lustres in the lodge window, when it suddenly seemed essential to go back to the shop. I might have forgotten something. Maybe I would think of something I ought to have remembered when I got there. I went round the roundabout, and drove on thinking hard. I shot the lights and an old woman on the pedestrian crossing looked up with an amazed face and nearly fell over backwards. I passed her with about three yards to spare but she had been looking forward to getting run over ever since horse-drawn buses had come off the road. I nearly passed a shop but noticed a campana-shaped vase in pale green out of the corner of my eye, and turned into the curb.

The lady of the establishment was hopping round in circles like a hobgoblin trying to make up her mind how much she would ask for the vase, and I was wondering whether like her I had forgotten to shave that morning, when I decided against the vase at any price. Her dentures chattered so brightly that I wanted to whistle the *Danse Macabre*. Her face went the colour of putty leaving two blotched spots on her cheeks and two dark holes where her eyes ought to have been and her lips trembled with irritation as I turned out of the place. I still couldn't remember what I had forgotten. The green vase was just an attempt to distract my attention, and I wasn't going to be put off.

I drove straight on to the shop. My manager was entertaining an Australian when I arrived, and she looked at me with the blank lack of recognition which meant it was a difficult sale. I went into the office and played with some consular invoices which were lying on my desk. She came in after a few minutes with her eyebrows raised.

'What brings you home so soon?' she asked.

'Anything?' I said.

'No – he wanted to see what would happen if he came in,' she replied. 'There's something about Australians which makes me think about little jugs.' I sympathised for a moment or two. There are people who come into antique shops looking for little jugs and they are very tiring to handle. It's best never to have a little jug on the premises. It only causes discord and it's never little enough. Or it's too little.

'Don't buy any little jugs,' I cautioned her, 'it'll only cause trouble.'

'I thought you were going to view that house,' she said, 'I never buy little jugs.'

'I remembered something,' I answered.

'What?'

'I forget.'

'Too many exciting afternoons at the auctions.'

'You're a manager, not a wet-nurse,' I reminded her gently.

There was nothing wrong with me that a good stroke of business couldn't put right. It was just that I was doing my best to keep a level head. You can't know what it means in this trade to get the smell of a large collection into your nostrils. You hear a rumour – you creep around after it – you speak to this one and drop that one and cut the other one in on a percentage. Then suddenly one bright morning when you've told yourself that the winter is over and the spring season is going to start, you hear: 'You know that collection?' You start up like a hound seeing a rabbit as big as a horse. 'Yes.' 'Burckhardt got it.' It's like falling into a pit. You say 'I should worry,' and you do.

Or you watch and wait and the time comes and you go after it. Its all been valued to the last halfpenny of profit. They want you to buy it, but they don't want you to have any blood left afterwards. You buy it high, and already the taste of it is sour. You hold it and hold it. Pay rent to house it, pay rates, pay income tax, pay and pay until the sight of all those bits of paste and pottery sickens you. Or yet again, you buy it so right that business is good for the rest of the year. Why shouldn't it be like that?

I was disgusted with myself. To hell with it, I thought, it's only another deal. It's only another little back-yard farce – me and a lot of other mongrels scrapping over a dustbinful of bones. In the end none of us would get them. All the old bones would, sooner or later, be cased up carefully and shipped to America. We lucky dogs got a little chewed up marrow for our trouble; the bigger animals on the other side were the real red meat eaters.

For years now the whole British antique trade had been singing *Passing By* to its best goods. The country was a canal zone and the canal led straight to the bottomless reservoir in America. We were just an old curiosity shop where the junk could be dragged out endlessly to the quaint accompaniment of a lot of anecdotes about the Duke of Clarence and this is the original Malmsey barrel a little worm-eaten, and how the Dowager Lady Dripping would be only too pleased to let you have her last tiara for a carton of Camels and six pairs of Du Pont nylons.

The Americans gave us their good hard dollars and took the lot, the big and the small, the right and the wrong, the Waterford chandelier and the bisque figure of a girl holding her skirt up. They took it away and built rooms round it and then houses round the rooms. It became part of their culture and why go to Europe when all the best pictures, sculptures, and genuine hand-made toasting forks are already in our American homeland? It was just darling, even if an occasional social misanthrope did call it conspicuous expenditure.

Once they had our bric-a-brac as a privilege and paid through their eyes, ears and noses for it. Now they bought it as merchandise in bulk, while we threw the profit away in riotous living in the provinces finding the next shipment for them. I was glad Joe Duveen didn't live to see something he started through to the bitter end – an American wholesaler knocking a dollar a time off the price of six Doulton chamber-pots in the Portobello Road. Joe was the last of the great nose-specialists. The dealer today was an old-fashioned bird of prey, a pterodactyl with more teeth than goods; about as adaptable as a four-horse chariot, he had all the chances of survival of a flying-pig. In twenty years time the few survivors would spend their lives buying up transfer-decorated lavatory pans for export – the latest fashion in wall lights.

You are a member of a dying profession, I told myself. You can either lie down and die, emigrate to America, or take a correspondence course in selling shoelaces. All God's chillun got shoes, and there might still be room in

34

the industry. I told myself to think it over and then give me a ring any time between eleven and twelve on the first Thursday of the month, if I wasn't too busy buying Wedgwood rooms, that is.

To hell with it.

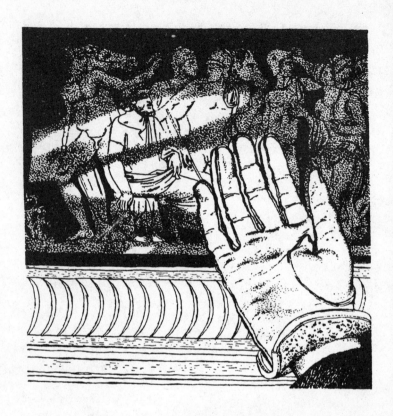

FIVE

WHEN I came round the next day I found myself driving along the North Circular Road at fifty-two miles an hour. It was a fine bright day and I by-passed the calls I should have made. By mid-day I was nearly there. I stopped just once to have another look at the map on the back of the catalogue, took a left fork on to a minor road, passed through a small village which looked as if it didn't know the steam engine had been invented, drove past a long high wall and stopped at a large pair of gates. They were worth about £120 and closed.

I rattled them for a while but they didn't seem to notice.

Then a man in shirtsleeves crossed what used to be a lawn dragging a tree branch behind him.

'Hey, George,' I called.

He looked up, not all at once, but drawing it out so as to make me think George wasn't his name.

'Can you spare a minute?' I shouted to him.

He put the tree down gently so as not to bruise it and walked over carefully. When he was right close to the gate I asked him if he had the key.

'Not locked,' he said.

'Bolted?' I asked.

He thought it out for a while, drawing his hand over his brown cheek so that it left a dirty mark.

'Yes,' he said.

'Does ten bob unbolt it?' I wondered.

He moved faster than he had since the free beer came up last hay-making.

I didn't want to waste time admiring the view. I didn't look at anything except the door of the house he told me was open. I pushed it hard and it creaked back slowly. It led into a stone corridor. I crawled around for twenty minutes before I found the room. I walked into six dining rooms, three sitting rooms, four parlours, and another half dozen different kinds of rooms, but there wasn't anything to make it seem worth while. Then I pushed open a pair of large mahogany double doors and walked into a room the size of Olympia. Wherever I looked there were Wedgwood plaques. My legs froze for a minute and then I lifted them up and threw myself in.

A deep frieze of blue and white plaques large enough to be called bas-reliefs lined the walls. The light in the room was good and I stood in the middle and counted them. I stopped after fifty-six and began to calculate what I should pay for them. Then I stopped calculating because the figures were beginning to frighten me. Someone had been pecking away at a light bracket on the wall and had left a ladder there. I grabbed the ladder and climbed up to get a closer look.

The plaque I was looking at was a Sacrifice to Pan. I rubbed some of the dust off with my hand. The surface had a slightly oily feel to it, a soapy texture. The figures were here and there a little mistaken in their poses and two of the bacchantes looked as if they had suffered serious amputations. The Pan himself had a face like an old goat you milk, not an old goat you run away from. But I could be wrong. I shifted the ladder to the other side of the room and climbed up to have a look at a Sacrifice of Iphigenia.

Now I couldn't be wrong. The Wedgwood Iphigenia was modelled by Paccetti in Rome under Webber's guidance. The dozen or so figures in it have the rhythm of a field of ripe corn when the wind touches it. In this one the figures looked as if they were leaning on one another to save falling off the wall. The Iphigenia bowed as if she had a bad crick in the neck, and if Paccetti had seen it he would have gone into the ice-cream business.

Every so often you just have to face life – look it square in the eyes and say: 'You win!' This was a time like that. I got off the ladder so as to say it in greater safety from the middle of the floor. I told those plaques they were a surplus broker's stock of grade ten French fakes. Then I went out of the room, my cheeks blushing with disappointment. I walked about ten yards up the passage and then came back. Nothing had changed except that I could now see at once they were fakes. I swore aloud and left them there to fool someone else. As I walked out of the house I counted the money I was saving, but I still felt as if I had just made a substantial loss.

Outside, the gardener was sitting on a tree trunk eating his lunch. I sneered at him. By rights he should have given me my ten bob back, but I wasn't going to be petty about this. I walked down to the gates wondering if anything had happened that morning at the shop, and telling myself the country air was doing me good. I didn't want to have any more expensive conversations with the gardener, so I went up to the lodge door and knocked a couple of times. I waited and then knocked again. I still waited and noticed that the gardener was watching me.

'All right,' I shouted to him, 'I'll buy it. There's nobody in. Right?'

He shook his head to save the wear and tear of saying 'No.' and I walked over to him.

'He won't open up,' he said.

'Will ten bob make him?' I asked. 'Or is he in a big line of business?'

'No,' my friend said, 'not even ten pounds would. He can't walk.'

I was saved the trouble of asking him to tell me the whole story, because the idea of the man in the lodge not being able to walk seemed to encourage him.

'Terrible thing – can't walk at all hardly – shakes like a leaf he does – can't talk even – old groundsman here – hasn't walked for years.'

'Hasn't talked either?' I asked.

'Hardly,' he said, and tut-tutted his way back to the log-rolling. He turned back once, 'Girl looks after him – red-head she is.'

I went back to the lodge but this time I didn't knock. I went round to the back door and walked in. It led into a shabby little kitchen, the kind of place which wouldn't stand up to a really good meal but made you think of porridge gone cold and cabbage water being saved for soup. A deal table was covered with a piece of American cloth rubbed through at the edges. A lightly boiled egg mashed on to a saucer and a mug of milk half empty waited for someone to come and clean them up. It looked like the old man couldn't eat or drink either. I walked straight through into the parlour.

Sleeping in a deep leather-covered stuffed chair was a

small old man. His mouth was open and he had no teeth. His breath came out in uneven shuddering gusts and his eyelids were only half dropped over his eyes. I could see their whites. I had to remind myself that you couldn't breathe if you were dead, because he seemed to be breaking the rule. Then while I watched he shook all over and started to wake up. But he stopped shaking suddenly and with his mouth closed tight now he went to sleep again.

I wasn't the man's doctor so I thought about leaving him to die quietly, when I noticed out of the corner of my eye something which made me remember. I went over to a Victorian what-not in the corner of the room and picked a piece of pottery off the bottom shelf. It was an old salt-glaze pew-group with the heads of both figures missing and a crack running across the base. For a while I didn't remember very clearly, and then as I stood there I suddenly knew that I had to find a pair of Whieldon figures somewhere. I poked about but I didn't find them. I didn't find a pair. But I found one, a beautiful fifteen-inch figure with a repaired head.

As I stood holding it in my hands I knew that the old man hadn't died. He was awake now and keeping one eye closed, he was watching me carefully with the other one. It was pale blue and full of water, but it seemed steady enough. Then he opened his mouth to speak and his eyes started to blink like a morse code transmitter. He got a few grunts out, but I pretended I didn't speak the language.

'Nice weather for the time of the year,' I said. 'Just having a look round the estate.'

He tried to get up and even managed to raise himself about three inches. But he sank back.

'You wouldn't happen to have a Portland in the house?' I asked him.

His eyes stood out like boiled sweets. 'A green Portland.' He tried to stand up again, and once more he fell back.

We were just beginning to get to know one another,

when I saw a red-headed girl in a yellow jersey go past the window.

'See you soon,' I said to the old man and slipped out of the back door. I heard him muttering and grunting to the girl as I left.

On the way home I told myself I was beginning to need a rest. A week at Bournemouth perhaps, at some quiet home for incurables.

That night I re-read some of my Wedgwood cuttings. I kept trying to avoid it but eventually I put them all away, and dug out that old tattered one which had been in my wallet for such a long time. 'Three salt-glaze pew-groups, a pair of Whieldon figures, and an old Wedgwood green copy of the Portland Vase.'

Except for two pew-groups, one figure, and the vase, I had located Mr Drage's lost collection. I started to tell my wife the whole story.

'And what then?' she asked.

'Then I took up flower-arrangement in a big way,' I told her.

That night I dreamt I was arranging flowers in a large green vase decorated with a cameo of a girl with red hair.

SIX

NOTHING much happened the rest of the week. I was
wondering whether to have the black edge printed round
the note-headings when a lunatic came into the shop and
with terrible intensity proceeded to buy portrait medallions.
It so happened that we had a lot of portrait medallions,
and the man was certainly a lunatic for he bought the lot.
When he had them parcelled up, his features relaxed and a
little blood came into his cheeks. I could see it had been a
hard fight, but he had won, and the cost was nothing to
reckon against the blessed relief he had gained. It was like
having an ulcer lanced. The poison was all drained away

and instead, he had a fine collection of medallions. Maybe one day they would start to poison him. Then he would get rid of them as quickly as possible and take to some other form of collecting. It takes all sorts to make a business.

On Saturday, I did an itinerant jewellery dealer a turn. He made a side-line of gold and dollars and I told him about someone who had offered me some dollars earlier that week. A legitimate trader hasn't much time for these little subtleties of business life, but this man was so cunning he often out-smarted himself just to keep in training.

He was the sort of man who got no satisfaction out of making a hundred on a straightforward deal, but a slightly illegal pound or two put him into a frenzy of excitement. When I told him about the dollars he started to sweat and his eyes turned into small flints behind his pebble glasses. He pushed his hat off his forehead, and couldn't get away fast enough. He left his suitcase behind, he was in so much of a hurry. It contained only about five hundred pounds worth of stuff, but making a few more pounds made him forgetful.

Sunday was a wet day. The boy and I built a stall out of some lathes and an orange box. We tacked a piece of red lino to the counter, and used an old twill sheet to make an awning. Then we found some chocolate cigarettes and some tins of sardines to sell to each other. We maintained the balance of trade all right, but business wasn't so good and by tea-time we were playing cowboys instead. All day long the baby was shuffling about the floor using a cunning technique he had invented as an excuse for not walking.

'Will that child ever walk?' my wife asked.

'He's saving his energy to eat with,' I suggested. I had to admire that baby. He kept busy organising the place, and without wasting a moment in idle talk, he managed to create enough work to keep a whole family employed for a week. At this rate he could take over the business in six months. A chairman of Great Universal Stores in the making.

That evening I was just about to have a good idea when I fell asleep on the settee. When I woke up my tongue was like a piece of *antico rosso* soaked in Parazone. Then I went to bed and couldn't sleep. Not sleeping was becoming a habit with me, and I began to wonder why. Whilst I was still wondering I fell asleep, so maybe I had broken the habit.

Monday, the first caller was the dollar collector.

'A fine favour you did me,' he whispered in a hoarse choked voice.

'Anytime – you would do the same for me.' I wasn't paying much attention. Then I saw he was unhappy.

'What's the matter?' I asked him. 'Did you lose on the deal?'

He did. There were tears in his eyes as he told me how he had bought the dollars for £140 and taken them straight to his contact. They should have brought £150, but the contact held them up to the light and shook his head.

'They were wrong,' the man cried, and he seemed to be all rolled into a ball like a hedgehog without any spikes on him. He tore the notes out of his pocket and threw them up into the air.

'They're wrong – counterfeit – all my years in the trade – what can I do?'

He was distraught and I genuinely felt sorry for him.

'Look on it as a business loss,' I suggested gently. 'Sometimes you make, sometimes you lose – that's business.' But he was suddenly calm, a sort of stupid kindness had settled over his face like a warm woollen blanket.

What now? I wondered. And then it came. As I had introduced him to the girl with the dollars, shouldn't I take half the loss? He didn't want to suggest anything, but how should he know whether the girl had made a separate arrangement with me? He wouldn't have taken the dollars, only I recommended the party and he knew me so well. And if not a half, perhaps a quarter. Why should he stand the whole loss? Weren't we friends? All right! He would settle for whatever figure I liked to name. He couldn't say fairer than that.

It was funny and I had to laugh a little.

'You have some funny ideas,' I said to him. 'Call in any time and we'll have a laugh together.'

His mouth opened and the smile left his face. His eyes were large now and innocent with tears. I gave him back his suitcase. It was funny and ridiculous, but it wasn't a good start to a day. After the little man left, I felt irritated and worried. It was his own fault and it had nothing to do with me, but I wondered what it meant. Business makes you suspicious. You look for signs everywhere, signs and lessons and morals. You may say that a little greedy man losing his shirt has got nothing to do with me. But you can't be sure. You can't be too careful. You can be too clever. You can't be clever enough. It's a bad lookout.

On the Tuesday, a taxi came to pick us up at eight o'clock. Sparta had a heavy old coat on which made him look like a draped wall. He had had trouble ungumming his eyelids that morning, and when he talked it was like the bark of an old wolf and didn't mean anything except he was there. I felt lively enough for a man who has spent the best hours of his night drinking lemon tea, and we didn't say anything until we got to the station. I paid the taxi and got the tickets. Abe Sparta always gave you the impression that you were his foreman, and when we got settled into a compartment he ordered me to get some papers; said: 'Bloody cold here,' blew his nose on a large khaki handkerchief, and sank into his big coat.

On the platform I had a feeling someone was watching me, and I looked around to see who it was. I could see no one I knew among the depressed morning faces. Picking up a couple of papers, I turned back to the compartment, when a husky voice called out, 'Here, Charlie!' It was a voice like half a dozen wrought-iron hinges rusting on an old gate. There was only one voice in the trade to match it. Turning round I saw the voice had no real competition. It was the man himself – Wendl, the break-up man. He had been an old-iron dealer in the days when my father had a stall, and many a big deal had passed between them, sometimes amounting to as much as thirty-five shillings. Now Wendl's was among the biggest of the break-up firms, but he was wearing the same green cloth cap he had worn years ago – or maybe now that he was a big business man, he had them greased specially.

'Hello, Mr Wendl,' I said, taking hold of a hand like a piece of old salted beef.

'How's your dad?' groaned the voice. 'Must be years – no, I'm a liar – saw him somewhere or other, sometime or other – can't remember – getting too old.'

'Not too old for business, Mr Wendl?' and I walked him back to his compartment.

On the way down the train, I glimpsed Armstrong from Welkin Street talking to two men in the corner of a compartment. It was becoming quite a party. I wondered if I should find that my uncle was driving the engine. It would have been nice to feel that I had a friend in a position of responsibility. As it was, I sat down in Wendl's compartment with a feeling that my goose was cooked and the boys were reckoning on having it for lunch.

Wendl puffed and groaned as if he was stoking up for a race with the *Rocket*. It was alarming, but I could see that it was only his way of sitting down and I didn't worry too much. Even if he did burst his boiler, I had my own troubles. So I gave him enough time to get settled and then I came straight to the point.

'You're not going to the big break-up, Mr Wendl?' I said.

'Why ask, Charlie boy, if you know?' he answered.

'It's certainly nice to see you again after all these years, Mr Wendl. I'll tell my dad. He'll be pleased.'

'But, I thought' – went on Wendl, 'Somebody told me – I don't know who – maybe your old dad. How is the old bastard?'

'He's fine, Mr Wendl. Just bought two tons of black pepper. You can imagine. He's very happy,' I said.

'So, as I say: what's in the break-up for you? Me, I'm a break-up man. Sashes, cornices, mantels, architraves, the bricks from the garden wall – I reckon them. But you! You going into break-up business?'

It wasn't that he was worried. His interest was ordinary human interest. He wanted to know whether I would be bidding against him. I went straight into what was becoming my routine.

'Look, Mr Wendl,' I said. 'I deal in English pottery.'

'Nice class of trade,' said Wendl, nodding his head and with a far away look in his eyes, as if he was giving the matter his earnest consideration. He was thinking how much he liked buying houses and pulling them down, and how pleased he was not to be in a nice class of trade.

'There's a room in this place,' I continued, 'with a lot of Wedgwood in it.'

Wendl held up his hand as if to stop me committing an indiscretion.

'You mean the panelled room?'

'Yes.'

The old man was silent for a while sucking on his teeth. Then he smiled as if I was his young grandson asking for a trip to the moon. He would have given it to me, only he wasn't in the shipping business. He spoke kindly.

'Look, Charlie boy,' he said. 'It's a nice room. Old pine, no rot, no faking, nice linen fold. Everybody wants it; like gold dust.'

He sank back as if he had told me more than he should.

'All I want is the Wedgwood,' I said, with a slight break in my voice.

'For my part,' wheezed Wendl, 'you can have it.'

'That's all I wanted to know, Mr Wendl,' I said, as I got up to go. 'Well,' I said, 'my dad will certainly be pleased to hear you're looking so well.'

'Wedgwood you can have,' he repeated, like God giving the sea to the fishes.

'By the way . . .' I was nearly out of the compartment but I leaned back '. . . who do you think's on the train?' I asked.

'Not the Chief Rabbi?' said Wendl.

'No,' I said. 'Another friend of the family : Abe Sparta.' I was out of the compartment, but I could feel the jolt as Wendl sat up.

'Who dug up that old bastard?' he croaked. 'The old cow-son thinks he can follow me? He should drop dead, the rotten thieving. . . .' He might have gone on a little longer, but this was just about where I had come in, so I left him talking to himself.

There are certain enmities in the trade which have no origin. A dealer who lives in one place hates a dealer who lives in another place. He doesn't know him out of the sale-rooms – whether he's an orphan; whether he's got children; whether his wife died giving birth. It isn't another human being he hates. It's another dealer. Maybe it's like two stags meeting. They fight because otherwise they wouldn't be stags. They don't think or count the cost, or ask what it means. The blood runs into their heads and flecks their eyes and their tongues go dry, and they fight.

Sparta and Wendl had come up fighting one another. They would fight over the panelling and one of them would get it while the other walked out with a white face and a racing heart, cursing himself for giving in and determined never to let it happen again. I didn't know who had beaten who the last time they met – they kept out of one another's way because even strong stags don't look for trouble – but whichever it was, I would be the first to congratulate him. After a battle, while the heat was still high, money meant nothing. Whichever bought the room, I would get the plaques at my own figure. And after all, they were good fakes, those plaques – they had a price. The two stags had a hyena on their tails.

By now, I was enjoying the situation. It was very funny and very clever and I was laughing to myself as I went up the corridor back to my compartment. 'You're a clever boy,' I told myself. 'Let the best man win and me as well.'

The train had started now. I passed Armstrong's compartment with a silly smile on my face, and he must have seen it because he called out: 'What are you so pleased about?'

I turned back. 'Hello, Armstrong,' I said. 'It's my sunny disposition.'

He was a tall, very thin, very long-faced man, who always wore the same mud-coloured suit. His eyes were like oil, dark and dead, and he had a hand like a cold fish-ball. He was an interior man, but that didn't stop him creeping into everything else, inside or out. He'd been in the game a long time and there wasn't much he missed. It never made him happy. He soaked up a fair amount of Scotch every day, but it only made his face longer and his hand more dead. I was willing to try again, but I would never get fond of him.

'Come in,' he said. 'We want to speak to you.'

I wanted to tell him it was only my first offence, and he shouldn't be too hard. He should let me off with a caution.

Inside the compartment, two smiles were fished out from the bottom of their spleens by a couple of American friends. They put them back quickly to save wear and tear.

'Sit down,' said Armstrong, the magistrate. 'Meet Mr Mindel and Mr Sweeting from the States. This is Mr ——,

I can never think of your name, Charlie – but Charlie is a bit of a specialist in his own way.'

It was a great build-up and Mr Mindel was pleased to meet me. Mr Sweeting took a tooth-pick out of his gum and waved it at me, so I suppose he was pleased as well.

'Well,' said Armstrong, 'what do you think of it?'

Mr Sweeting put the tooth-pick back. Mr Mindel was looking at me through half-closed eyes and fishing for that valuable smile of his again. He nearly found it.

'A very nice compartment,' I said, 'but I must be going.'

'Look, Charlie,' Armstrong said, 'I know what you're after, and you know me.' I nodded that I knew him. 'I wouldn't stand in your way in the ordinary run of things, but Mr Mindel and Mr Sweeting here haven't come all the way from the States for nothing, you know.'

Mr Mindel and Mr Sweeting tried to look like a pair of early colonial pioneers. Their jaw lines almost emerged from their necks, but sank back through lack of practice. Their eyes were like steel and with a little more tempering would have thrown off a spark or two. But they still looked like a couple of dealers to me.

'No,' Armstrong went on, 'we want that room, Charlie. We're going to rip it out and pack it up and ship it straight out to California.'

'We surely are!' said Mr Mindel.

'That's right!' said Mr Sweeting.

'So why?' pleaded Armstrong, 'why waste your time, Charlie, and get nothing for your trouble? Leave it to us and we'll see you all right.'

'Play ball with us,' said Mr Mindel.

'And we'll play ball with you,' said Mr Sweeting.

They were a wonderful combination and I could have clapped my hands with pleasure. I sat down next to Armstrong.

'That's the idea!' he said. 'What the hell – we're all in the trade, aren't we – why should we fight?'

And in this atmosphere of jollity, I sat and talked about life with my three new friends – prices in America; the cost of shipping; how much Mr Sweeting made; then how much Mr Mindel made; then how much Armstrong made. I told them the story about the man who didn't speak for fifty years, and when he did finally stand up to say something, it turned out to be: 'Life is a big fish.' Everyone thought this a very fine saying, until the local teacher came right up close to the old man and asked him. 'How can you seriously suggest to us that life is a big fish?' 'All right,' said the man, 'so it isn't a big fish.' And he sat down and never spoke again.

Armstrong brought down his little attaché case and gave me a piece of chocolate. Mr Mindel gave me a packet of Luckies. Mr Sweeting gave me some chewing gum and a tooth-pick. They would have given me the business if we weren't all dealers together. As it was, we were friends, only they were going to have the room, and I was going to be paid out.

'Don't think I'm being small-minded about this,' I said, 'but how much?'

'Don't be silly, Charlie,' said Armstrong. 'We're not dealing small – there's a clear pony in for you.' He took out his wallet. 'And you can have it now.' He started to count out five fivers.

'Well,' I said, standing up, 'thanks for the chocolate and cigarettes, but I must be running along.'

Armstrong looked hurt. 'What's the matter, Charlie? Isn't twenty-five enough?'

'Look, Armstrong,' I told him, 'there's a lot of money in that room I'm not going to make, if I do as you tell me. Do you think it's enough?'

I took fifty after a little more friendly discussion and left after shaking hands all round. I mused on the idiocy of a life which tosses you money when you don't work for it, and a bellyful of promises when you do.

Back in the compartment Abe Sparta was asleep. I didn't wake him up. He had a hard fight ahead of him and I wanted him to be in a fit state for it.

SEVEN

THE position an hour before the auction was due to start was this. I had been paid fifty pounds not to bid for anything by Armstrong, Mindel and Sweeting. I had an arrangement with Abe Sparta to buy the Wedgwood in the room from him if he bought the room. And if Wendl bought it, he was prepared to sell me the Wedgwood as well. But it wasn't Wedgwood and if I got it at all I had to get it at shipping price – for nothing. It was still two-to-one that I would get it for nothing, unless Armstrong made an arrangement with Sparta or Wendl. But dealers like Wendl and Sparta can ship as fast as they can buy, and they were too big to be both paid off. They were also too proud to buy and then go back with nothing except more money in their hands. After all, dealing for these men isn't just making money. It's a lot of other things as well – other things not so easily arranged – feelings having nothing to do with profit and loss accounts. But if the worst came to the worst, I could go back that night with a good day's wages for my trouble. It wasn't a bad break-up so far as I was concerned.

Sparta woke up a few minutes before the train was due in. He looked about him with a vacant expression as if trying to remember where he was. He looked at me once or twice without recognising me, and then again. 'Oh, that's where you are,' he muttered. 'Where are we?' We were coming into the station, and I suggested that it might be best if we get a taxi first and then something to eat. My stomach was self-supporting at the moment and I wanted to make some small contribution – a dry cheese sandwich for example. The old man was still a little bit vague. 'Leave it to you, Charlie,' he said. Then he came round. 'So long as we don't get there too late. No,' he went on, 'we'd better get straight there and see what's happening. Says here in the catalogue light refreshments will be obtainable.'

As we walked to the taxi Sparta looked back and saw Wendl a few yards behind. His face went the colour of borsht.

'That old bleeder Wendl. Did you see him?' he growled. 'Follows me about the old rat.'

'Here's the taxi, Mr Sparta,' I said.

He got into it still cursing Wendl. I saw Armstrong and his friends get into another taxi but I don't think they saw me. Wendl didn't take a taxi. He was the sort of dealer who knows all the bus services and isn't ashamed to save money by using them. He passed us as we got into the taxi and I said in a loud voice: 'A lift? Well, yes thanks, Mr Sparta, it's very nice of you.' But old Sparta wasn't interested. 'You see that mean old bastard, Wendl? Wouldn't take a taxi if he had to go on his hands and knees.'

It was an untidy countryside with a lot of trees looking very underfed, and greyish grass which no self-respecting cow would give a second look at. We passed a few blank-faced farmhouses, one of them a decayed Jacobean relic with a large muddy field in front of it. Some sick looking cows were stuck knee-deep in the mud, but no one worried. Abe Sparta showed no interest in the rural scene except once when we passed an open-shaft iron ore mine.

'What's that?' he asked, and when I told him, he replied: 'That sort of business is all right for Wendl, he's an old-iron man. But I'll tell you something for nothing. The timber round here isn't worth a light for cutting. I never did see such a miserable lot of overgrown weeds. Trees, you call 'em?'

He glared at me like I was selling trees. Then we came up over the crest of a hill and below us we could see the gables of a fine house. Sparta had the driver stop for a while so that we could admire the view. We got out of the car and stood by the road looking down on to the house, and we didn't say anything.

The morning was just getting into its stride, and the place had a look of having been there for ever. The stone toned into the colours of the fields, and the house sat there as if it had grown up with the hill. Sparta was staring down at it all and I was telling myself how there wasn't a dealer in fine things who could help responding to beauty. I felt a glow of satisfaction when Sparta said quietly, 'That, Charlie, is a very fine house – a very fine property.' He was quiet again except for a sigh. 'Yes,' he said, 'it's a beautiful house. It would be nice to have the breaking of it.' Nothing could stop him being an Odessa lumberman. He loved trees but only when they were chopped down.

We were coming to the house now and Sparta leaned forward in his seat. We drove into the grounds through the iron gates. Now a board saying SALE THIS DAY was tied to the gatepost. I noticed a little smoke trickling out of the chimney of the lodge and I thought I caught a glimpse of a vase on the mantel over the fire, but maybe it was a mirage.

The house itself seemed larger than before. Four corinthian columns formed the centre entrance. The wings swept round on each side to form a crescent. It must have been magnificent in the old days, but murder on the feet – the sort of place where you need a bicycle to get from the sitting room to the nearest lavatory. Now the façade had that diseased look which means the break-up isn't far off. A lot of stucco trimming had cracked away revealing the brick beneath, but whoever bought those bricks would certainly have to work to drag them out. That place had been built. Built like a monument to stand up for a long time. It would have gone on standing up, too, if it wasn't for the demolition dealers. It wouldn't have done anyone any good, of course, and in a hundred years or so it would have disappeared, but it would certainly have stood up for a while longer than the determined men who were, even now, getting their tackle ready to tear it to pieces.

The main doors were open today and inside it was dead cold with that bitterness which only large long-empty houses have. I put my collar up and followed the old man to the room. On the way we passed some sheet lead which had been ripped off the roof. Sparta stopped and stared at it. 'You see that?' he said. 'The bastards have pinched the lead already – lead! You know how much lead there is there?'

I said, 'No.'

'A lot – a lot.' The old man shook his head at the criminal idiocy of a world which entrusted lead to people other than Sparta. He rapped here and there on the walls as we went along, just for practice.

We walked round to the room. The doors were open today and as soon as we walked in, Sparta began to examine the panelling. The plaques were still there and they looked terrible. The ladder was still there, too, but I noticed that all the light brackets had disappeared. Sometimes trifles do walk before an auction begins. I climbed up the ladder to make it look real. When I came down, I nearly tripped. It depressed me to be on top of so much cheapness.

I tapped the pocket with the ten fivers in it as I walked back to Sparta.

'What do you think of it?' I asked him.

'All right,' he said.

'I only want the Wedgwood if it's cheap,' I told him. 'Wrong colour.'

'You want it cheap?' he said, still bent over the panelling. 'Don't we all?'

'I was just telling you, Mr Sparta,' I said.

'Don't worry, Charlie,' he said. 'I'll manage.'

As I left the room, Armstrong and the Americans came in.

'How do you like it?' Armstrong said.

'You buy it,' I told him. 'It's good.'

Then I went to the refreshment room for that sandwich.

EIGHT

THE position when I took my first bite of the cheese sandwich, was this. The auction had just started. I didn't want
to buy a thing. Wendl wanted the panelling. Sparta wanted
the panelling, and Armstrong wanted the lot. I looked at
my watch. I could be back by the early afternoon, but
somehow I wanted to see the thing through. I wanted to
know whether anyone else would see that the plaques
weren't right, and I didn't want to miss the big fight either.
I finished my coffee and ordered more. There were two or
three local dealers hanging about, but no one I knew. Then
Wendl came in and sidled over to me.

'Have a cup of coffee, Mr Wendl,' said. 'Warm you up.'

'Does Abe Sparta want the room?' he answered, as I handed him the cup.

'As a matter of fact he does, Mr Wendl.'

Wendl took a long drink before he spoke again. Then he asked me to come into the garden for a breath of air.

The canteen was in the old kitchens, so we went out the back way towards what used to be the stables. Wendl shuffled along.

'We walking home, Mr Wendl?' I asked him.

He didn't answer until we were about fifty yards from the house. His voice was pitched so low that nearly all the rasp had left it, and it sounded almost gentle.

'Listen, Charlie,' he whispered. 'I'm one of your dad's oldest friends. I knew you when you used to sell stamps on the corner of your old man's stall. I want you to do something for me.'

'You know I'd be pleased to do anything I can for you, Mr Wendl,' I said.

So after telling me what Sparta had done to him over the past twenty years, he finally came to the point. He didn't want to bid. Sparta was only there to make him pay. I should bid for him. Of course, he would look after me.

My ethical position was deteriorating fast. I had been paid not to bid by one – I had cancelled a joint arrangement to buy with someone else – I had decided not to buy for myself – and here I was being asked to buy for Wendl. If I bid after agreeing with Armstrong not to, it would be bad for my reputation and I would have to give him back ten fivers I had grown fond of. If I gave him back the fivers and bought for Wendl, it might be worth more than fifty to me, but Sparta would be annoyed – and he was my landlord. But if I *could* bid, it would be the funniest deal of my life.

The room was lot number 178 and it didn't come up till after lunch. That gave me an hour or so to think of something.

'Look, Mr Wendl,' I said. 'Mr Sparta is my landlord. I haven't got a lease and I have a family to keep sheltered. I think he might not like it if I bid against him.'

'I'm ashamed of you,' Wendl said, 'for being frightened of a great ox like him. Come on, Charlie – you'll do me a turn?'

'I'll see you in about half an hour, Mr Wendl, and let you know,' I said.

'What's so difficult you should have to think it over for so long?' he croaked after me, but I was already back at the canteen door.

There was Armstrong drinking Scotch with the Americans. He said to me with misery in his voice, 'Lovely room, isn't it?' It must have been his third double and it was beginning to depress him.

'Sparta's mad about it,' I said.

'Who? Abe Sparta?' he asked, swallowing the rest of his drink.

'Yes,' I said. 'He wants it badly.'

Armstrong gathered his friends to him. 'This isn't so good, boys,' he said. 'Sparta's a hard man to do business with.'

Mr Sweeting said, 'Yeah?'

Mr Mindel didn't say anything.

'Just thought I'd let you know,' I said.

'Very nice of you, Charlie,' Armstrong said with sincerity in his voice. 'I appreciate it.'

'That's all right,' I told him, 'you've been fair to me and I want to be fair to you. Did you see Wendl was here as well?' I added.

'Wendl,' Armstrong explained. 'He's not interested in panelled rooms. He's strictly demolition.'

'He happened to mention he could use a panelled room,'

I said. 'I think he's always wanted one and he loves the Wedgwood in this one – thinks it just makes it.'

'It sure does,' said Mr Mindel. 'I sure want that room.'

Armstrong blinked his eyes in irritation.

'Well, you're out anyway, Charlie,' he said with an edge of threat on his voice.

'That's right,' I said, 'it's all yours – and Sparta's – and Wendl's. Goodbye.'

'Just a minute, Charlie,' Armstrong called, 'don't be in such a hurry always. You know Wendl, don't you?'

'Very old friend of the family,' I said.

'What about Sparta?' he asked.

'Even older friend of the family.'

Armstrong looked at his associates and then gave me a long straight glare. 'Can you fix something?'

I shook my head. 'No one can fix those two old dogs,' I said. 'Certainly not me. Why don't you ring it with Wendl? He might be interested.'

'Will you speak to him?' Armstrong asked.

I said I would and went back to find the old man, feeling that at least my fifty was safe.

Wendl agreed without a struggle. He didn't want to have to fight Armstrong's friends as well as Sparta.

'Will you bid?' he asked.

'I don't know yet, Mr Wendl,' I said. 'I'll tell you.' I thought for a while. I looked at the catalogue and then I went off to find Sparta.

I searched through the rooms until it felt as if my feet had taken frost-bite. The auctioneer was carrying the bidding with him from room to room, and he sold a nice piece of rotten cornice moulding for ten shillings as I passed him. He was a big, fresh-faced man with riding breeches and high boots, and he looked as if he'd like to get back to the pig market. I couldn't blame him. He was surrounded by a small crowd who looked as if they would garotte him for sixpence. The pigs were more generous.

I found Abe Sparta out in the grounds looking up at a fine oak. He had an abstracted look on his face whenever he looked at trees.

'Not gone yet, Charlie?' he said.

'No,' I said, 'I thought I'd hang around to see what was happening. I just spoke to Mr Wendl.'

'What did the grisly bastard have to say? You know, Charlie,' he ran on, 'you should be careful who you mix with. He can give you a bad name.'

'He hasn't come for the room,' I said, 'I know that. Well, I'm off now, Mr Sparta. See you tomorrow.' I walked towards the gate.

'Hey, Charlie!' the old bear shouted. 'Come back a minute.' I came back a minute. 'So what does he want?' Sparta said.

'He didn't say, Mr Sparta, but he asked me when lot 206 should come up.'

Sparta took his dog-eared catalogue out of his pocket and licked his thumb. 'Here it is,' he said, 'Lot 206: the painted metal stairs finely wrought and so on.'

'Yes,' I said, 'that's it.'

'I'll just have a look and see what the old bleeder's up to,' Sparta said, and he scuttled back to the house.

When he button-holed me a quarter of an hour later his face was grey with suppressed excitement.

'He wasn't far out the old bleeder,' he said. 'You know what those stair-rails are made of?'

I didn't know.

'Lead,' Sparta whispered, 'and it's not catalogued.'

'I thought it might be something like that, Mr Sparta,' I said.

'Charlie – you've done me a good turn.' He gripped my shoulder hard as if I had just saved his little boy from drowning. 'I won't forget.'

'What about the room, Mr Sparta?'

'To hell with the room,' he said. Who wants a pine room?'

'I might buy it myself if it goes cheap,' I remarked carelessly.

'You have it, Charlie, I won't bid against you. What do you think of that cunning old bastard letting me think he wants the room?'

'Well, I hope you get the stairs, Mr Sparta,' I said.

'Thanks, Charlie,' he said, 'and Charlie, tell your wife of course she can leave the big pram in the shed.'

'That'll please her,' I told him, and I went back to business.

By lunch time the situation had clarified. First and foremost, I was in the clear. Then, Armstrong and Wendl were going to ring the room. Sparta wasn't interested, but only I knew it. He wasn't going to leave those stairs until they were sold. I had to laugh. I had picked on the stairs just because I reckoned a metal merchant ought to be interested in metal, and because Sparta always thought of Wendl as a metal merchant. If Sparta got them and they were lead, good luck to him. If Wendl didn't get them and he didn't know they were lead it wouldn't hurt him. I was squared with Armstrong, but they were giving me a share in the knock-out because I was going to do the bidding. Now there was only the question of the local opposition, the possibility of there being a high reserve on the room, and the danger of the auctioneer trotting the bidding. Even a pig-seller knows how to pick imaginary bids out of the air if his ten per cent is suffering.

There had been no excitement so far in the bidding. It was all routine stuff, and everyone was talking about the room and trying to guess what it would fetch. I couldn't see anyone who looked like a buyer though, and it seemed we would have it pretty well to ourselves. I wanted to find out if it carried a reserve. I introduced myself to the auctioneer.

'It'll be the room you're interested in?' he said, after looking at my card.

'You certainly sum things up quickly,' I said to him. 'I did come down to buy the room. It would have been very nice if it had been right. Still, that's how it is in this game. You never know until you see it.'

He looked puzzled. 'You mean to say it's not right?'

'Not a piece there that's right,' I repeated. 'All French copies. If you had one of them out I could show you.'

'Come along to the office will you?' he said.

As we walked down to the butler's pantry which they were using for an office, he asked me: 'You specialise in Wedgwood, do you?'

'That's right,' I said.

He shook his head. Back in the office he had a broken plaque. He handed it to me. I turned it over and handed it back.

'If it was Wedgwood it would be solid. This is hollow. If it was Wedgwood it would be dull. This is shiny. And anyway it would be impress-marked. This is junk.'

'We thought it would fetch a lot,' he said.

'It may,' I told him, 'there are plenty of mugs who don't know the difference. If you're lucky, there might be a couple here today.'

'But it's no good to you?' he said, a little desperately.

'Only if it goes reasonable – not if the reserve is high. And not,' I looked straight into his eyes, 'not if it's trotted.'

'We don't do that sort of thing in the country, you know,' he said, hurt.

'I'm glad to hear it,' I said.

'And nothing's reserved very high. It's all got to sell or be pulled down, you see – it's purely a demolition job – d'you see?'

I could see that he was frightened the London dealers would cry off in a crowd and his sale might go to hell.

'Well, maybe I'll hang around and see what happens,' I said.

'Yes, do,' he urged, 'I'm sure it will be all right.'

'Thanks,' I told him. 'I can see you're going to be fair about it.'

I was getting to be a first-rate canvasser. Maybe I should go in for politics.

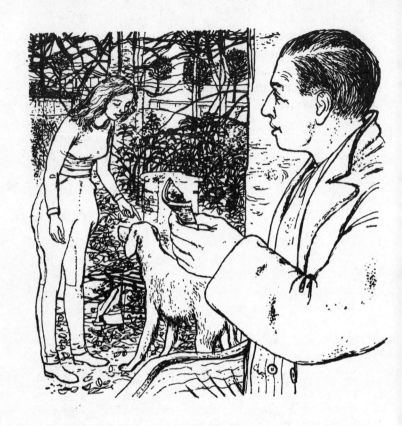

NINE

I COMMUNED with nature during the lunch recess. I took a glass of beer and a meat pie out into the garden, and sat on the trunk of a tree down by the porter's lodge. I broke the crust off the meat pie and examined it. It was like a piece of heavy parchment, and I wondered what good it could do me to eat it. I threw it high into the air to see if it would take off. Then I took the solid wad of meat out and studied that, too. It looked like an old composition floor the damp had attacked. I nibbled a little of it just in the way of experiment. It tasted of nothing I wanted to put my finger on. The rest of the crust slipped away from it like a plaster mould, and I threw it in the same direction. It fell about the same place and there was a scrambling noise as if it had started to dig its way back into the earth. Then a red setter jumped out of the bushes and stood stock still a couple of yards from me. Thinking that at least someone would make a profit on the pie, I offered him the wad of meat. He came up to it slowly, as if he had experienced this sort of disappointment before.

'Go on,' I told him. 'Eat it up – it's only another old red setter. Dog eat dog,' I told him. 'Eat it up. Enjoy it.'

Then, because the dog still seemed uncertain, I tried to make a little polite conversation.

'How's business?' I asked him. 'What do you think of the room?'

Then, because he seemed new to the game, I thought I'd take him into my confidence.

'Don't touch the room,' I told him.'I know about these things. Don't touch it. It's dead wrong.'

That seemed to convince him of my good faith, and he came up and licked at the meat.

'Yes,' I told him, 'you look like an honest dog to me, and I wouldn't like to see you go wrong on that room.'

He took the meat into his mouth confidently now, as if he had earned it.

'You should give me the meat,' I told him, 'after all, think of the money I'm saving you.'

The dog didn't answer, so I stopped wasting my valuable time on him.

A woman was standing by the bushes a little nearer to the lodge. She was wearing jodhpurs and a yellow sweater, and her figure didn't suffer by it. She had red hair, cut carelessly, and her face was pretty without being anything out of the ordinary.

'I don't mind you talking to my dog, but I'd be grateful

if you wouldn't feed him,' she said. 'Drop it, Rover!' she told the dog.

But he wasn't going to give up so easily. He pretended to be deaf as well as dumb and finished the meat quickly in a great gulp.

'Sorry,' I said, 'but we were having a quiet little talk about business and he said he hadn't eaten since breakfast.'

'Yes,' she answered, 'I heard. What makes you say the room is no good?'

I looked at her. 'You don't look like a dealer,' I said.

She laughed, and it was a nice performance – a low, long note which could shatter your backbone if it really tried.

'No,' she said. 'My grandfather was the groundsman here in the old days. He has the lodge. I look after him because there's no one else.'

'Nice quiet life,' I suggested.

The red setter was being a good boy now. He kept twining like a snake between her legs. It didn't seem to me that he was wasting his time.

'Won't you take a seat?' I asked her.

'It's lovely here, isn't it?' she said, sitting down.

'Yes,' I said, 'it's got a nice atmosphere of decay – and I like the way the herbaceous border's gone tropical and the trees haven't been pruned and the bushes haven't had a haircut in years. It's nice and wild, but the break-up boys will soon tame it. In three weeks, there won't be a wild strawberry left.'

'It's sad, isn't it?' she said.

'I suppose so,' I said. 'Though it'll only fall down if it's left. This way at least someone makes a profit – men make a living – rents are paid and children get new toys and wives new hats.'

'Are you going to pull it down?' she asked. 'You don't seem like a demolition contractor.'

'I'm glad you said that,' I told her. 'Destruction is foreign to my nature. I wouldn't harm a slate on its roof. I came for the room.'

'And yet you say it's no good. I think it's very lovely, but I suppose you only care about its value.'

She was beginning to treat me like a knocker – as if I was calling on her to see if she had anything to sell today madam. I glanced at my watch. It wasn't too late to begin a little course in aesthetic appreciation, and she was a nice class to teach.

'Now look,' I told her, 'I'm a dealer and I care about what things are worth because that's the way I make a living. If I stopped caring, then I wouldn't make a living. You don't want my family to starve, do you?'

She laughed as if the idea was funny.

'People have different ideas about what's beautiful, and I wouldn't contradict a single one of them, but in my experience when something's really beautiful, it's also rare. If it's rare, there are people who want it just because it's rare. They don't care about its beauty. It's just something on one else has got so far as they're concerned. Or, it's an investment, or a way of hiding money from the income tax. But don't blame me if I sell to these people. I'm only responsible for the rarity and beauty of the thing I sell. I'm not responsible for their reasons for buying it. If I only sold to people with a nice sense of beauty, I'd be president of a debating society, not an ordinary ignorant dealer. As for that room,' I said, 'there isn't a piece of Wedgwood in it. It's all fake stuff let into some nice panelling, and for my part it kills the panelling.'

She looked depressed now, and I felt sorry I'd opened my mouth. It was better she should stay ignorant and go on seeing beautiful things. I might be doing a lot of harm by telling her the facts of life.

'What's the matter?' I asked her. 'It doesn't belong to you, does it? What do you care how much it brings?'

'To tell you the truth,' she said, after a while, 'Grandfather is to get a little out of what the place fetches, and he needs it badly.'

I looked at her and she blushed.

'I'm surprised at you,' I said. 'Here you are, telling me all about beauty, when what really worries you is what price it's going to fetch.'

'It's not for myself,' she snapped back. 'I'm not going to make anything out of it.'

'It's like that for all dealers,' I said. 'All they get out of it is the fun of the fair. The profit's to pay the rent collector and the milkman.'

Now don't think I had forgotten what I was sitting on that log talking philosophy for. It's always nice to put over a good line of sales talk to a red-headed client, but this time I was setting the right atmosphere for breaking and entering the lodge again. And this time I would have my own guide.

'Look here,' I told her, 'I'm the only dealer here who knows the stuff's no good, and I haven't learnt what I know in order to educate the masses. The room will fetch good money and Granddad will get his slops for another five years.'

That cheered her and she got up to go.

'Has your grandfather got any bits and pieces he might like to sell?' I asked her.

'Well,' she answered, 'he does have a few bits and pieces now that you ask.'

I was away now after the hare, and she didn't look like a pretty girl any more.

'I'd like to see them very much,' I said. 'You never can tell.' I got up to follow her.

'I'm afraid Grandfather's asleep now,' she said. 'He suffers from agitans and he's very ill and I don't want to wake him. Could you come this afternoon and then I can ask him? He can hardly talk, poor dear. But I can understand him.'

I could come and we said goodbye with lots of smiles. I saw her to the door and shook hands with her to make her feel that we were already in business together.

As I turned to go, I could have sworn that there really was a vase on the mantelpiece. I didn't want her to see me looking through the window, so I walked back to the house. But I could have sworn there was a vase over the fireplace.

TEN

THE arrangement was that I should buy Lot 178. The little crowd following the auctioneer around had been belching its way through indigestion and a few dismal lots which were the overture to 178. Then when they came into the room, a hush fell over the assembly as if they were in chapel and cared for that sort of thing. Armstrong and the Americans were out of the way looking unconcerned in the far corner, but I could feel their eyes drilling wormholes in my back. Sparta wasn't about. He was frightened the stairs might walk and he wanted to keep on their tail.

Wendl was over by the window picking his nose as if nothing else mattered. I couldn't see anyone who looked like a bidder, and for a moment I entertained the dealer's old hope that maybe he'll buy on the first bid. Lately I've only seen it happen with a bundle of rotten curtains and a Britannia metal plate-stand, but it could happen here, too. I wondered if the girl in the yellow jumper would come to watch, but she wasn't about.

The auctioneer was giving a short speech on the history of the room and how fine it was and how lucky we were to be buying it. Just as he finished his story and said 'Now, gentlemen, shall I say five hundred to start?' the girl came in. I bid him fifty just to show how much his sales talk was worth. She looked fresh and small – a flower on a rat-infested rubbish dump.

The auctioneer was speaking after the slight murmur which followed my bid.

'Now, gentlemen, I appreciate a joke as much as the next man, but let's have a serious offer, if you please. The whole room, mind you, including these magnificent Wedgwood plaques.'

He caught my eye as he said it and threw me a roguish twinkle. But no one bid.

'Speak up,' he shouted. 'A serious bid, if you please.'

'All right,' I said, 'sixty.'

Then he looked over my shoulder and said, 'Seventy, am I bid? Thank you, seventy.'

I couldn't see who was bidding. Either someone was having a go while the figure was small, or he was trotting.

'Eighty,' I said.

He took another bid from behind me.

'Ninety,' I told him.

Then we bid in twenties.

At two hundred and forty we were still bidding, and my hands were sweating. At three hundred I stopped to get a nod from Armstrong. I looked round. There was a slight buzz around the girl over to the right. As I looked, she nodded her head.

'It is yours, madam,' the auctioneer said gallantly.

She was bidding against me. Why? Who for? What was all the talk about back on the tree trunk? Maybe I should have let her teach me the business. Wendl now gave me four quick nods.

The auctioneer was saying, 'Going, at three hundred,' and leering at me.

'Three fifty,' I said, to show I was serious and glanced over at the girl. Her expression meant nothing. It was just a dish cover and no one could say what she had on the dish.

She ran me up to four twenty and then turned on her heel smartly and walked out without a word.

'Thanks for your help,' I called after her neat, cunning little figure. 'That'll be enough now, sir,' I said to the auctioneer.

'I think so,' he said, with that happy leer, and knocked it down to me.

We met outside. 'Not such a bargain,' Wendl said.

'Leave it to us, if you like, Wendl,' said Armstrong.

'Let me finish, Mr Armstrong, if you please,' answered Wendl. 'I was going to say, not such a bargain, but what can you do?'

'All right then,' Armstrong said irritably. 'Let's find an empty room somewhere, knock it out, and get home.'

I could see he was dying for a drink. Wendl had stopped picking his nose, but he looked as if he was still thinking about it. Mr Sweeting had come to the point where only chewing his toothpick would quiet his nerves. Mr Mindel kept bleating, 'It's a lovely room. It sure is a fine room,' as if he was trying to sell it to himself.

For my part, I couldn't stop wondering about the girl. Even if it wasn't my money I was throwing away, it still hurt me to be run. I would rather have left her the room.

What the hell could she do with it anyway? Maybe she wanted it to put the vase in – if she had a vase.

We found a room in the servants' quarters not much bigger than a large cage. We made a ring, all of us bidding, me with Wendl, and Armstrong with the Americans. Wendl put the room up at four twenty and bid another ten. We went round twice in tens, making another hundred on the price. Then we went round once more, putting another fifty on. Then Wendl bid a hundred more. He didn't want to waste time messing about, he said. That made the price two hundred and fifty more. Then Mindel got very excited.

'We want that room,' he snarled – if a sheep can snarl. And he bid another hundred. He seemed to forget we weren't playing stud poker, although Armstrong was looking worried. The price was now three hundred and fifty more, and it was enough. Wendl looked unhappy and said: 'All right, you can have it.'

'We'll pay out back in town,' Armstrong said.

'No,' said Wendl, 'we'll pay out here before Charlie transfers the lot.'

'What's the matter Wendl?' said Armstrong. 'Don't you trust us?' He didn't like the room so much now.

'I trust you,' said Wendl, 'but business is business, so let's get it settled.'

They paid out Wendl in cash for both of us, two-fifths of three hundred and fifty – one hundred and forty pounds in new fivers.

'All right, Charlie,' he said, 'transfer the lot to these gentlemen,' and we all trooped down to the auctioneer's office.

Afterwards Wendl said to me, 'Charlie, greed is a terrible thing. Just think what that room cost those men because they were greedy.'

He gave me forty and put the rest back in his pocket.

'So you made a crust today, Charlie?' he said. 'Remember

me to your dad,' and went off to catch the bus back to the station. I asked him did he want to buy anything else in the break-up, and he said sadly : 'It's taken care of, Charlie, don't worry.'

He hadn't given a damn for the room. He had bluffed good money into his pocket out of the pockets of Armstrong's friends, and that was all he wanted.

I went back to have another look at the room. For all that money, it looked worse than terrible. Armstrong and the Americans were running about measuring it up and telling one another how lucky they were to get it.

'Wendl certainly caved in,' Armstrong said to me, for the benefit of his friends.

'Yes,' I agreed, 'there were tears in his eyes when he left.'

ELEVEN

I T was three o'clock and the position was that the party was over and I had ninety pounds in my pocket. Like Wendl, I didn't care a damn for Wedgwood rooms. All I wanted to do was to go to every break-up in the country. In two years I would be able to buy enough Savings Certificates to settle down quietly and live on the interest. But I wasn't really serious. I knew that it was a fluke. It would never happen again like this, and on the whole, I wasn't sorry. There's a lot of luck in business, but it would be terrible if there was nothing but luck. It would be demoralising, and the competition would make life impossible. There are a lot of lucky people about and every one of them would be a dealer, and if that happened, who would there be left to sell to? The trade would go out of business if it was all luck. There had to be something else as well. What it was I didn't know, but it had to be some thing.

I was sorry the girl in the yellow sweater should have treated me like that after our talk, but I was going to take her at her word and see what her poor old grandfather had besides agitans. I walked over to the lodge after telling Sparta I'd be back for the taxi at four. He was too interested in the stairs to worry about me. Looking at his glazed old eyes it seemed to me that he didn't have very long to live. He couldn't think of more than one thing at a time, and thinking about that one little thing took up all the breath and blood and life he had left in him. He couldn't have been much older than Wendl, but he had used himself up faster and with endless, senseless fury, while Wendl paddled along saving money on bus fares and quietly never missing a deal. Sparta was almost a hulk. It just wanted another cold winter or a really bad deal to put him out of business. All that silver-gilt up in his safe would come out, and while his wife looked at it through red-rimmed sightless eyes, maybe it would cross her mind that the fire was burning low and they were out of coal again.

As I walked over the untidy grass and the muddy drive down to the lodge, I was inclined to be philosophical. What did it mean, anyway, this break-up, or anything else for that matter? To begin with it meant people dying alone and so quietly that no one noticed it until probate was granted. But even that wasn't the beginning. It started with a man living. He put a few stones together and crawled between them. Finally he built a house with a hundred rooms and into every room he put a thousand bits and pieces to look at and think about. He was just about to explain exactly what all these bits and pieces amounted to, when, unfortunately, he died. They were lost – it couldn't be helped. The man's life was in them and when he died they had nothing left to live for – until the dealer came along and gave them meaning for the lives of other men. The dealer was the ring-master in a dream circus – he flicked his catalogue and presto, another routine. As for him, the dealer, the Autolycus of the auction-rooms, he never owned a thing in his life, and he knew it. The objets d'art, the objets vertus, the bijouterie and the pots, they all passed through his hands and into history. Who knew better than he that nothing is given, that everything passes, the woods decay? He was the ultimately human being. He resigned himself to making a profit. Whether or not grandfather had a vase worth buying and selling was the only question.

I knocked at the door of the lodge, and after a couple of minutes it was opened. It was the red-head, but she was wearing a dress now. It was a light dress of a brilliant blue colour and for a moment, after that red and blue hit me between the eyes, I could find nothing to say. She smiled at me as if auctions couldn't be further from her mind, and said: 'How nice of you to come. I was just about to make a cup of tea. You will have one, won't you?'

I said, yes, I would have one, and she led me into the small parlour.

The old man was sitting by a small bamboo table in front of the fire. He was bent over the table, smaller than life. A little dull white hair was plastered carefully over his skull, and his face was shrunken and very pink. His eyes stood out like marbles, and swivelled a little when he spoke. The only way he could stop his hands shaking was to keep them on the table. He couldn't move very much, and every time he opened his mouth, I thought the effort would spin him out of his chair.

I could see that conversation was out of the question until the girl came back, so I told him what a nice little place he had here, and how nice it was out, and what a nice girl his granddaughter was. He gulped every so often and I took it to mean that he agreed with me. But until the girl came back, I didn't take my eyes off the vase standing on the mantelpiece. When she did come back, it was difficult to know which to watch. If the vase won, it was only on points – points of information with which I happened to be familiar.

It was a Portland vase about ten inches high, and generous in its proportions, decorated with a pure white cameo on which the shading was as delicate as the carving on an antique gem. The side facing me showed Pylades, the rope dancer, approaching the daughter of the Emperor lying on her sick-bed with Cupid flying over her, and Galen, to the other side, bearded and very stern, pointing out that the only trouble with the princess was that she was sick of love. It was the usual Portland story, but this time it was told with so much genius that my heart skipped a beat every time I looked at it.

And that wasn't all. The white cameo was laid upon a silk-smooth jasper of a green which had never existed before. It was the translucent green of deep sea-water, a green with more green in it than any other colour, but with every other colour there, too. And there wasn't a doubt in the world that it was an early copy – nothing later than 1795 could have had that precision and clarity, that quality of sheer genius which spoke to you clear from the other side of the room. And yet no green jasper Portland was ever made in the period. There's no mention of it anywhere. They were all black, or blue-black. First Portlands don't exist, and if they do, they aren't green. But this did, and it was the greenest green in the world.

I talked to the old man about the weather until the girl came back with a tea-tray with two cups and saucers on it.

'Grandfather mustn't drink tea,' she said. 'Now have you had a nice chat?'

I said, 'Yes,' and the old man gulped again, and she busied herself pouring out the tea.

'I was surprised to see you bidding at the auction today?' I said.

'Wasn't it fun?' she cried, putting the tea-pot down.

'What did you want with the room?' I asked gently. 'Are you going into business with your grandfather?'

'Mr Pilkington, the auctioneer, gave me five pounds to nod my head at him until he waved at me. Wasn't it nice of him?' She was being very sweet about it.

'It certainly was,' I said. 'You cost my friends a nice packet.' Pig-dealing hadn't hurt that auctioneer at all, I thought.

'Oh, good!' she said. 'Grandfather – you should get a nice little present out of the sale – isn't that nice?'

Deaf as he was, the old man caught the sense of that and made a sudden jerk which almost knocked the bamboo table over. He put his heart and soul into it and managed to say 'Good,' but it was hardly worth the effort.

'I was very glad, too,' I said. 'I bought it for some fellows who would be very happy tonight if they knew their money was doing your grandfather good.'

Then I talked about the vase and said what a pretty green it was.

'Grandfather had me fetch it out of the attic the other day. He wanted it left on the mantelpiece so he could see it all the time. I didn't even know he had it.'

She let me pick it up and I noted there was no mark on it, except for a small manganese pencil X on the inside rim. It was solid body and it felt like silk. The cameo in the base was the most perfectly gem-finished work I had ever seen.

'It's very pretty,' I said. 'Would your grandfather like to sell it?'

The old man was watching all this palaver very closely, keeping his hands well on the table to stop them shaking. His eyes were practically out of their sockets, but only he and I knew why. This girl was saying: 'You wouldn't mind, would you, Grandfather? I knew you would be pleased.'

The old boy was doing his best to have a stroke. But she understood him and knew he was pleased.

'What is it worth?' she asked.

'Well,' I said, 'there are all sorts of vases of this pattern, but this one is nicely made and I like the colour. I might pay a very good price for it.'

The old man was shaking away, trying to tell her to throw me out. But I held on to the vase and kept smiling. Ninety pounds had fallen into my pocket that day. 'I'll give you eighty pounds for it,' I said.

When she recovered, she told the old man and he jerked for a while, trying to tell her, 'No'.

'He's trying to say he's very grateful,' she said to me, 'Mister . . . I don't even know your name.'

'Drage,' I said. 'Name of Drage.' I was looking at the old man. He made a convulsive effort and rose up shaking upon his feet.

I counted out sixteen fivers, smiling at him the while.

'Thank Mr Drage, Grandfather,' the girl said.

He moved and pushed the table over, scattering the five-pound notes.

'He's so excited, Mr Drage,' the girl said, and she put him carefully back in the chair.

I watched his eyes. It wouldn't have been impossible for him to add murder to his crime sheet. As it was, what could he be convicted of? Had he stolen the Drage items all those cold years ago? Stolen them thinking, 'A promising young man in service deserves a better start — I'll pawn them and open a tobacconist shop.' And did he suddenly realise that now he had them, all he could do was to get fond of English pottery? Or had he gone in for a little quiet receiving and found the goods didn't sell? Whichever way it was, what was he worrying about? Now I had the worry and he had sixteen fivers to buy himself a nice silver-plated coffin.

She found a box for me and I packed the vase up, carefully stuffing newspapers round it. She was very happy and couldn't stop thanking me for being so nice. She was a nice girl and I could have spent a long time talking to her without getting bored.

'I'm sorry about bidding against you at the auction,' she said, as I was about to go. 'I feel very ashamed.'

'Don't be,' I told her. 'You look after your grandfather always like that.' After this shock, he was going to need careful nursing until he could work up enough energy to steal Mr Drage's vase back again.

She had eyes, that girl, and lips, and the only colour that would ever bring out the full beauty of her hair was the green of that Portland.

The whole jungle was never as green as that. The whole jungle which looked after the tiger, sometimes let the bird of paradise, the flash of light under the trees, take a quick flight round the festering mangrove swamps. Even if it has to finish up on a hat at the world première of a film about the fall of man, let the bird take flight once in a while. It won't alter anything, although even the tigers will give it a glance as it passes. It may not show a profit now, but one long dark night when there's only one good tooth left in his decayed jaw, an old tiger will think about it.

'Goodbye,' I said to the girl, 'and thank you.'

'What for?' she asked, 'you've been very kind.' For one moment there was only a vase between us. It was a moment of deep sentiment, so I did my best.

'For having such red hair and such green Portlands.'

She laughed on that long, low note again, and I kept a tight hold on to my box to stop the sound hurting the vase.

TWELVE

I GOT back late that night. I was very tired and happy in a sad kind of way. The hall light was on and the flat was quiet. I took the box into the kitchen and unpacked it. I put the Portland on the table and sat in front of it for a while, watching it silently. I made some tea then, and ate a piece of cherry cake I found in a tin. Then I drank tea and watched the vase for some time. I didn't think about anything. I just looked. Then I put it away in the sitting room, and turned the bath on. While the bath was running I went back to the sitting room and looked at the Portland again. Then I had a bath slowly and nearly went to sleep in it. I took another look at the Portland before I went to bed.

As I got into bed my wife stirred and woke up. She switched the light on.

'Is that you, Charlie?' she asked faintly.

'No, It's Abe Sparta,' I said.

'You're late,' she said.

'Yes. It's been a long day.'

'What did you do?' she asked, yawning.

'I sold a room. Then I didn't buy it. Then I did. Then I sold it again. Then I bought a green vase.'

'Is that all?' she said. 'It sounds very tiring.'

I pressed down into the pillow. 'No,' I said, 'it wasn't tiring. Just a little confusing.'

'Is it a nice vase?'

'It's nice.'

'Well, that's good then. I'm going back to sleep now. Goodnight.'

'Goodnight,' I said, kissing the back of her neck. 'Oh yes,' I remembered, 'Abe Sparta says, of course you can put the big pram in the shed.'

She sat up. 'Now that is nice of him,' she said. 'Why didn't you tell me before?'

'I kept it as a surprise,' I said.

I turned round to go to sleep, but I kept wanting to go back and look at the vase again.

About two o'clock, I got up. I put the vase in the middle of the table. Then I looked at one side for a while; then the other side. Then I walked round it from left to right; then I walked back again from right to left.

A Kid for Two Farthings ◆ ◆

Illustrated by James Boswell ◆ ◆ ◆ ◆ ◆

For my Grandfather
and his
Great-Grandsons

ONE

It was thanks to Mr Kandinsky that Joe knew a unicorn when he saw one.

He also knew that the Elephant and Castle was the Infanta of Castile, a Spanish princess. He knew that Moses was an Egyptian priest, that the Chinese invented fireworks, that Trotsky was the best revolutionary, and that pregnant was going to have a baby. Joe was six, and thanks to Mr Kandinsky, he was educated, although he didn't go to school, for he had to look after his mother till they came to Africa.

His father said to Joe when he was still five, 'Look after mother till you come,' and Joe said he would. Then he went down to talk to Mr Kandinsky in the basement. No teacher knew what Mr Kandinsky knew, about the Elephant and Castle, that is, and the unicorn. Soon after, Joe's father went to Africa, with two suitcases and a Madeira hat for the hot weather.

Joe lived upstairs at number 111 Fashion Street. There was a bedroom and a kitchen, and the kitchen had a fireplace and a gas stove, but no sink. The tap was at the top of the first flight of stairs, and Mr Kandinsky used it, too. The lavatory was in the yard at the back and smelt of Keatings Powder. Mr. Kandinsky lived in a room on the ground floor, and had a workshop in the basement. The workshop had a window below ground level, and there was an iron grille over the pavement for the light to come through. In the little area outside the window were bits of newspaper and an old hat and a sauce bottle, and Joe wondered how they got through the iron bars, because it was a top hat and the bottle was the tomato sauce kind with a wide bottom.

'We ought to look, Mr Kandinsky,' Joe said one day, 'because maybe there are some pound notes and sixpences mixed up with it all.'

'Joe,' replied Mr Kandinsky, 'who has pound notes or even sixpences to lose in Fashion Street?'

So the window was never open, except in the summer it was lowered a few inches at the top, and a lot of dust came into the workshop.

Mr Kandinsky was a trousers-maker. In the workshop he had a sewing-machine, and a bench with the surface all shining from where he and Shmule pressed the trousers. In the fireplace were two big gas rings with two big goose irons beside them. When the cloth was soaked in a pail and spread over the trousers, and the hot goose iron pressed on top, a great cloud of steam arose. Mr Kandinsky always said it was bad for your health and the worst thing in the tailoring, even bringing on the consumption. On the wall were three hooks with large brown-paper and cardboard patterns hanging on them. On the mantel were two boxes with flat pieces of white tailors' chalks in them, and hundreds of cloth patterns in books, and dozens of reels of cotton.

Mr Kandinsky had two pictures. Over his bench was a big print of a lady with her head bowed sitting on top of a large grey-green ball. Her eyes were bandaged and she was holding a broken harp. Joe thought the lady was a street musician who had been in a car accident; she was crying because her harp was broken and she couldn't live by singing any more. Mr Kandinsky looked at the picture for a while and said, 'You know, Joe, maybe you're right. But what about the ball she is sitting on?'

Joe thought it over while Mr Kandinsky hand-stitched a pair of fine worsted trousers, but in the end he had to give up. Then Mr Kandinsky told him:

'This ball is the world and this lady is Hope who is always with the world. She is blindfold because if she could

see what happens she would lose hope and then where would she be? What this broken harp means, I don't know.'

'Maybe it's a bit of another painting,' Joe said.

'Maybe it is,' said Mr Kandinsky, 'who knows?'

'Who knows?' repeated Joe, because he liked the way Mr Kandinsky said things. 'Who knows?' he said again, putting his head to one side, opening his hands and trying to lift his eyebrows.

The other picture was a brown photograph of an old man with a long beard and side curls, and bushy eyebrows, and a great curved nose with curved nostrils. This was Mr Kandinsky's father. 'A pious man, Joe,' Mr Kandinsky said, 'very respected in the village, the finest coat-maker in the whole country.'

'Not a trousers-maker?' asked Joe.

'Certainly not,' said Mr Kandinsky, 'he was a great man and he would never lower himself to be a trousers-maker.'

'Why aren't you a coat-maker, Mr Kandinsky?' asked Joe.

Mr Kandinsky, who could answer all questions, replied, 'Because my wise father put me to trousers-making, thinking that Kandinsky and Son would be able to make complete suits. And you know what that means, Joe? It means bespoke tailoring – no more jobbing for other people. You can be an artist, not just a workman, somebody can send you sackcloth you will make it up into a pair of trousers. But it was not to be. It was a dream, Joe. Never mind. Life is all dreams – dreams and work. That's all it is.'

After this talk, Joe nodded at the photograph of Reb Zadek Kandinsky when he came into the workshop. The stern eyes looked past him into the future, a lost future of Kandinsky and Son, bespoke tailors. The curved nostrils turned disdainfully away from Mr Kandinsky, the Fashion Street trousers-maker, well-known in the trade, but not in the same class as his father, a master-tailor, who died cross-legged on his bench, stitching the reveres of the first coat

94

he made in London. 'May he find his place in peace,' Mr Kandinsky said, 'that last coat was beautiful I tell you, Joe, beautiful.'

'I think your trousers are lovely, Mr Kandinsky,' Joe said, to cheer Mr Kandinsky up.

'Thank you, Joe,' he answered, 'I will make you a pair of blue serge trousers.' And he did, a real pair of trousers, with turn-ups, and a cash pocket. Everything, even proper flies.

The whole house was Mr Kandinsky's, not his, but he paid the whole rent and Joe's mother gave him ten shillings every week. He was an old friend and the arrangement was made before Joe's father went away. Mr Kandinsky could spare the room. 'I am the only Kandinsky extant — which means the last Kandinsky,' he told Joe. Joe thought how it must make you old to be the last one extant. He looked at Mr Kandinsky. He was very old but his face wasn't worn out. In fact he had much more face than Joe, and Joe wasn't extant at all, having both his mother and father as well as Mr Kandinsky. Joe kept a pet in the back-yard, a day-old chick, which sometimes lived for two or three weeks. After Mr Kandinsky told him he had no people he called his pets Kandinsky in memory of that family.

At Friday night supper, Mr Kandinsky and Joe's mother talked about Africa and Joe's father and what he was doing there and how soon Joe and his mother would go out to him.

'You know, Rebecca,' Mr Kandinsky said, 'your fried fish is not just fish — it is manna from heaven.'

'You are always paying me compliments, Mr Kandinsky,' Joe's mother said.

'And why not, Rebecca?' said Mr Kandinsky, 'you are the prettiest girl in the whole East End.'

'Girl,' said Joe's mother, and laughed, blushing so that she did indeed look quite pretty.

'Isn't she pretty, Joe?' asked Mr Kandinsky.

'I think you are very pretty and nice,' Joe said to his mother, although she had stopped smiling, and her face looked sad and not so pretty.

'For how long?' she said, 'how long is anyone pretty?' Mr Kandinsky cleared his throat which meant he was going to say something important. Joe looked at him, waiting.

'You are pretty as long as someone loves you, Rebecca,' he said, 'and so many people love you that believe me you are very pretty. Look at me. I am ugly, and old, but even I am pretty when someone loves me.'

'I love you, Mr Kandinsky,' Joe said. 'One morning you will look quite pretty.' Mr Kandinsky put his hand on Joe's head.

'Thank you, Joe,' he said, 'I feel a little bit prettier already. To celebrate I will have one more piece of this wonderful fish which the miracle of your mother's cooking has made as sweet as honey.' Mr Kandinsky, Joe thought, never got tired of fried fish.

'So what does he say in his letter this week?' Mr Kandinsky would ask. 'How is the Kaffir business?'

Joe's mother read parts of the letter out aloud, with Mr Kandinsky stopping her every so often by raising his hand and asking a question. Then they would discuss the matter for a few minutes before she went on reading. Sometimes they were very long letters, full of business details, five gross of steward's jackets, twenty gross denim trousers, add ten per cent for carriage costs, a hundred pound company, five pounds paid up, salesman's commission on a hundred ex-army bell tents, and so on.

These letters were full of excitement, with little stories of Kaffirs drinking their white beer and singing, or Kaffir boys met late at night marching down the street beating a drum, and Joe's father walking in the road, otherwise they would beat him up. The long excited letters had money in them. As Rebecca opened them, the corner of a five-pound note, and once a ten-pound note, and always a few pounds, would be seen. Unusual, exciting notes they were, not ordinary but African money. But other letters were very short. There was no message in them for Joe or Mr Kandinsky at all, and for Rebecca just a few words. These were the bad letters, and if Joe asked too many questions after they arrived, his mother's face would look at him as if she couldn't see, and if he went on asking questions, it would suddenly begin to tremble and then she would cry, hugging him and making his face wet with her tears.

In the mornings Joe's mother went to the Whitechapel Road where she worked in a millinery shop. She trimmed hats with bunches of artificial fruit and flowers, and Mr Kandinsky said she was the best and most artistic hat-trimmer in the millinery trade. Because she didn't come home until the late afternoon, Joe ate with Mr Kandinsky and Shmule at twelve o'clock, downstairs, in the workshop. Mr Kandinsky never allowed Joe's mother to leave something cooked for them.

'I am an old cook myself,' he told Joe, 'although your mother is the best cook in the world, Joe, I am not saying anything against her cooking.'

Mr Kandinsky cooked on one of the gas rings in the workshop. On one of them a big goose iron was always heating, and on the other a large cooking pot with two handles bubbled quietly all morning long. Into the pot Mr Kandinsky threw pieces of beef or a small breast of lamb, with plenty of onions and pepper and salt, and some large potatoes. Or a large marrow bone cooked with carrots, or mutton cooked with haricot beans. At quarter to twelve Joe went up the street to the baker on the corner to buy three onion rolls. Then they all sat down with big enamel plates full of steaming stew, eating and talking. Joe liked Mr Kandinsky's cooking very much. 'The best cooks are men, Joe,' said Mr Kandinsky. 'Some men cooks get thousands of pounds from the Kings of Europe for cooking dinners no better than this.'

Mr Kandinsky talked a lot, but Shmule was often quiet. Shmule was short and broad, and very strong. He had bright red hair which curled into small flames, although after a haircut it was more like a piece of astrakhan. His skin was pale and his eyes grey, and every Saturday he spent the whole day at the gymnasium developing himself. Developing yourself was the only thing Shmule wanted to talk about, which was the reason why he said very little, because Joe was too young to develop himself much, and Mr Kandinsky was already too old. Occasionally Mr. Kandinsky would bring Shmule into the conversation by saying, 'You got a new muscle to show us?'

Shmule at once took of his jacket. He rolled up his shirt sleeves and clenched his fists and bent his elbows till large knots appeared everywhere. Sometimes he took his shirt off as well. He put his arms over his head, and enormous bands of muscle stood up on his back and chest. Joe clapped and Mr Kandinsky called Shmule 'Maccabeus,' which means 'The Hammer,' and was the name in which Shmule wrestled. But once or twice Shmule tried a new muscle and though it came up a little distance it fell down straight away. Then he blushed from his forehead to his neck, and went into a corner to practise.

Shmule was going to be a wrestling champion, which meant he had to beat Louis Dalmatian, the Stepney Thrasher, Turk Robert, Bully Bason, and the dreaded Python Macklin. He didn't have to beat them all at once but even one at a time was enough, especially the dreaded Python Macklin, who had broken limbs with his powerful scissors grip. Shmule showed them the scissors. He took a chair and fought with it on the floor, twining his legs round it and pressing hard, explaining all the while, until one of the chair legs cracked and Mr Kandinsky shouted, 'The furniture he breaks up!'

'A chair I can mend,' said Shmule puffing and blowing, 'but supposing it was my leg?'

So between Shmule and Mr Kandinsky, Joe learnt a great deal about the world. Though he was a bit young, Shmule taught him the position of defence and how to give an uppercut. But it was Mr Kandinsky who told Joe all about unicorns.

It was the afternoon that Joe's chick Kandinsky was found dead on its back, legs in the air, a ball of cotton wool and two matchsticks. Joe was worried because he did everything the day-old chick man in Club Row told him to do, and yet the chick died. Mr Kandinsky suggested that perhaps it could happen that Joe wasn't a natural-born chicken-raiser. Chickens just weren't his speciality. Maybe he should try a dog or a lizard, or a couple of fish. This made Joe think why not write to his father for a big animal, because naturally small animals only have small lives and naturally they lose them more easily.

Mr Kandinsky had been studying Africa in some detail since Joe's father went there, but the parts in the book about the gold mines and diamond mines were not as interesting as the chapter called the Fauna of Central Africa. He was, consequently, in an excellent position to advise Joe on the habits of larger animals.

They discussed the lion with some hope, because many cubs have been trained into good pets, but lions only eat meat, and where would they get enough to feed it? You couldn't fool a lion with vegetable stew; even Mr. Kandinsky's cooking would only make it angry and then there would be trouble. The giraffe was nice, but with such a long neck, you couldn't get it in the house. A zebra is only a horse with stripes, and horses you can see any day in the street.

'Maybe,' Joe suggested, 'maybe my father could send a unicorn.'

'A unicorn is a public house,' Shmule said, looking up

from a small book he was reading, *The Principles of Judo*.

'Don't show your ignorance on the subject, Shmule,' Mr Kandinsky said. Then he told Joe about unicorns.

'Every animal when it was made by the Almighty was given one extra-special present,' said Mr Kandinsky. 'The squirrel was given a wonderful tail to hold on with so he wouldn't fall from the trees; the horse was given strong fine legs so he could run fast; the lion great jaws; the elephant a trunk so he could take a shower whenever he felt like it, because an elephant is so large, how else could he keep clean? But the unicorn got the most special present of all. He was given a magic horn which could cure anything anyone was ever sick from. It could grant anybody's wish – straight off. And this horn consequently was worth £10,000 cash on sight, anywhere in the world. Don't ask me why the unicorn got this present. Someone had to get it, so why not him? Anyhow, he got it and no one else. But because of this very gift unicorns became so scarce you won't even find one in the zoo, so it is in life.

'At one time unicorns were common as cart-horses, wherever you went in the streets you would see half a dozen. In those days no one was poor. You needed something so all right, you just reached out your hand and there it was, a glass of lemon tea, a new hat. Then, when people became poor, all the unicorns had their horns stolen and sold. You can imagine what that did to them. Could a lion live without his jaws, could a squirrel swing from the trees without his tail, could an elephant go on without a shower-bath, could I eat if I stopped making trousers? Of course not, so how could a unicorn live without his horn?

'Ah, Joe, they died in their thousands the lovely unicorns. They gathered together in dusty yards and at the bottom of those streets which lead nowhere. They nuzzled one another for comfort, and closed their eyes so as not to be reminded of what they had lost. Their fine white coats became spotted, their beautiful sleek muscles slipped away into twisted sinew. They pined, they shrank, they faded, they died, and their death was sad for they had been eaten up by poverty, swallowed in the darkness of a pit with no bottom, so that no one ever saw them again.'

Mr Kandinsky sighed as he bent to throw his cold goose iron on to the gas ring. He looked at Joe with big eyes and sighed. 'This was the pity of it, my Joe,' he said. 'The unicorns passed away, but poverty was still in the world, poverty and sickness. Strong men have wasted away, beautiful girls have grown ugly, children have been lost before they could yet walk, the unicorns are all gone and yet poverty is still here. Don't ask me why. What do I know?' He sighed again, then put his hand on Joe's shoulder, pressing so as to feel the small fine bone. 'Never mind,' he said, 'sometimes in spite of everything, a child grows well, a man goes from strength to strength, a woman's face does not fade. In the same way some unicorns must have lived. They were the clever ones. They saw how things were going and didn't waste time blaming men or cursing life, or threatening God, or any other foolishness. Instead they came forward and said to the rest, "Listen friends. If we don't do something soon there will be no unicorns left in the world."

' "Be quiet," some of them shouted, "can't you see we are too unhappy to do anything."

' "Don't be blasphemous," others cried, "it's the will of God."

' "Don't interrupt us when we are crying," others said, "it is the only thing left for us to enjoy."

'But some gathered together to escape, some with hope in their hearts, some with doubt, a few with the spirit which does not care either for hope or doubt. These said, "Living means waste, but let who wants to live, live."

'One old unicorn who had been told about Africa when he was a baby had never forgotten. He told them, and to Africa they went that very night. In Africa they are today, although their terrible experiences made them careful about being seen by men, so that nowadays you don't see them so often. But they are even bigger now, and stronger even, and so fierce they fight at the drop of a hat. Without doubt, Joe,' said Mr Kandinsky ,'without doubt, Shmule, you wrestler,' he said, 'there is absolutely no reason why there shouldn't be unicorns in Africa.'

'What do I know?' asked Shmule.

'Could I get a unicorn into the house?' Joe asked.

'A small unicorn,' Mr Kandinsky said, 'certainly. There is no reason why a small unicorn couldn't be got into the house. Would you like another spoonful, Joe?' He stirred the carrots in the saucepan on his gas ring so that a great cloud arose.

TWO

AFTER Kandinsky the day-old chick died, Joe went to the animal market, because if you wanted a unicorn, the best place in the world to look for it was Club Row.

Joe had his own way of walking through the market. It made it much larger if you started in the middle where the herring women fished salted herrings out of barrels with red hands, dipped them in water and cleaned and sliced them thinly with long thin knives. From there you walked up to Alf, the singing-bird man, then cut round the back, coming through to the other end where the dogs were. But if there was something you wanted to buy it was much better to start at one end by the singing birds and walk through, looking carefully at every stall.

Alf, the singing-bird man, came to Mr Kandinsky for repairs so he knew Joe and always spoke to him, even if he was busy selling someone a canary. Alf was against day-old chicks as pets. He pulled his light brown overall coat down, pushed his cap back from his eyes and told Joe when he bought Kandinsky, 'You ain't doing that chick no favour, Joe, taking him away without his mother, alone, he doesn't know how to give a peep-peep yet, putting him in a box with a drop of water and a handful of straw. That rotten day-old chick man should be put in a box himself, the louse, selling chicks to anyone with a sixpence. A chick like this needs his mum or a special hot-box; he don't just grow up any old how any old where, he must have special care, he shouldn't catch cold.' Alf turned to a fat lady with a big grey fur round her neck. 'That canary, lady,' he said, 'is such a singer I should like to see better.'

'He don't appear to be singing much just now,' the lady said, taking a handful of potato-crisps from her bag and crunching them. 'Tweet-tweet,' she said to the canary, spitting a few little bits of potato-crisp at him, 'tweet-tweet.'

'Here, Oscar,' Alf said, because all his birds were sold with their right names on small red certificates. He whistled softly to the bird. Oscar turned his bead eyes towards Alf, listened for a moment, and then began to sing.

'Lovely,' the fat lady said, finishing the crisps and brushing her fur, 'how much for the bird?'

'That Oscar,' Alf said afterwards, 'I had him nearly a year. And he started to whistle softly to a dark gold canary.

Near Alf's stall there was a jellied eel stand with a big enamel bowl of grey jellied eels, small bowls for portions, a large pile of lumps of bread, and three bottles of vinegar. There were also orange and black winkles in little tubs, and large pink whelks. People stood around shaking vinegar onto their eels and scooping them up with bread. A little thin man in a white muffler served them and sometimes dropped a large piece of eel on the ground. Behind the stand a very fat man with a striped apron and an Anthony Eden hat waved a ladle in his hand and shouted, 'Best eels, fresh jellied, buy 'em and try 'em, eels.' Over the stand a red white and blue banner flapped. 'The Eel King,' it said. The King himself never served.

Opposite the Eel King was a red barrow with dark green water melons, and a white enamel table top with halves and slices of melon and a large knife. Joe pretended he couldn't make up his mind whether to buy some jellied eels or a slice of melon. He watched people eating eels and shaking vinegar on them, and then looked back at the large wide slices of red melon with glossy black seeds bursting from them.

In the end he bought a twopenny slice of melon and pretended it was jellied eels, scooping the red flesh with his teeth and saying 'Blast' and 'Bloody' when the seeds dropped

to the pavement. Some of the seeds he saved so that when they were dry he could crack them between his teeth and get the thin nuts inside.

While he scraped the thick skin of the melon, Joe watched the Indian fortune teller who wore a turban and sold green, yellow and red perfume in small bottles. Whenever a woman bought a bottle of perfume the Indian looked at her strangely. 'A little moment, dear lady,' he said, 'a little moment while I look into the bowl.' He looked darkly into a large glass bowl which turned purple or orange, and sliding his hand beneath brought out a small envelope with a fortune in it; the pavement all round his stall was covered with torn envelopes. Once when the market finished, Joe kicked his way through the empty boxes and newspapers past the Indian's stall. He saw him counting sixpences into piles, and putting them into small blue bags, but the bowl looked like an ordinary bowl for goldfish. An Indian girl who wore a long blue silk robe was packing the bottles into boxes on a barrow. When the Indian pushed the barrow away, the girl walked behind him; they went to the bottom of the street and turned away into the darkness under the railway arches, back to India.

The Sunday came when Joe had saved enough of the six-pences Mr Kandinsky gave him every week for helping in the workshop, to buy a unicorn, should one appear. Mr Kandinsky was always busy on Sunday mornings, and he hardly noticed Joe leave. He was arguing with a customer who wanted a zip fastener on his trousers, something to which Mr Kandinsky could not agree.

Joe ran quickly through the crowd to the singing-bird end of the market. Alf was talking to a budgerigar and a tall thin man with a sad face. The bird wasn't replying, but every so often the thin man said,'It's no good, Alf – it's no good,' till at last Alf put the cage down. Then the bird suddenly said, 'Hello' and Joe said hello back. The thin man looked sadder still and left, and Alf said, 'Talks better

English than I do – hello, Joe, what are you after? No more chicks remember.'

'Do you know where I can find a unicorn, Alf?' Joe asked.

'Try down by the dogs, Joe,' Alf suggested. 'Hello,' the bird said again.

'Hello,' Joe replied and started towards the other end of the market.

On the way Mrs Quinn, the hen woman, called him over.

'Joe,' she said, 'tell your mother I'll bring the eggs over meself tomorrow.' She was holding a fat hen which squawked as an old woman pinched it and complained. 'If you don't like the bird for the love of St Patrick leave it,' shouted Mrs Quinn in Yiddish. 'So tell your mother now,' she said to Joe.

'Do you know where I can buy a unicorn, Mrs Quinn?' Joe asked.

'What do you want with heathen animals?' she answered. 'Get yourself a nice day-old chick.'

'That day-old chick man, the louse,' Joe said, 'he should be put in a box.'

'Will you leave the bird alone now?' screamed Mrs Quinn at the old woman who was still pinching its bottom.

'There's no harm,' Joe thought, 'in at least having a look at the chicks.'

At the stall, hundreds of them were running about in a large glass enclosure with a paraffin lamp in the middle of it, all squeaking like mice. When someone bought them they were put into cardboard boxes with air-holes, and the squeaking became fainter. It was a pity they had such small lives.

'Another one already, cock?' asked the chick man.

'Not today, thank you,' said Joe, 'I'm not a born chick-raiser.'

'You got to know the trick of it, cock.'

'I'm going to buy a unicorn this time,' Joe said.

'You do that,' the man said, 'you do.' He bundled two dozen chicks into a box and tied it up with string.

Just about the middle of the market, near the herring women, was the fritter stall which also sold hokey-pokey ices and sarsaparilla fancy drinks. The smell rushed up so thick from the great vat of frying oil that if you stood nearby for a while you had a whole meal of fritters. The hokey-pokey man called out, 'Get your hokey-pokey, penny a lump, the more you eat the more you jump,' but Joe hurried on. He passed the cat-lady with her basket of kittens mewing, and the long line of hutches where the rabbits were always eating. He waited for the bearded sandwich-board man to shout at him, 'The wages of sin is death, repent lest ye perish,' because he was studying to spit when he spoke. 'Sthin – death,' Joe spluttered as he hurried on.

The dog-sellers mostly stood in the gutter or against the bill-hoardings holding a puppy in each hand and one in each pocket. They didn't say anything unless you patted a pup. Then they told you he was a pedigree Irish retrieving elk-hound, his mother was a good house dog. A few of them had cages with bigger dogs in them, and one or two men just stood around with four or five dogs on leads, trying to make them stop walking round in circles and jumping at people. There were dogs with short legs and long tails, and dogs with short tails but long ears. They were all dogs all right, all yelping and barking, just dogs.

Joe walked right to the end of the dog-end of the market, hurrying past the man who bit off exactly at the joint dogs' tails that needed lopping, to the very last man standing by the arches under the railway. The four sixpences and four pennies in his pocket clinked and three men tried to sell him pedigree pups, but the last man stood by the dark opening of the arches without speaking. He held a large white rabbit under one arm, and in the other hand a piece of tattered string, and at the end of the string, a small unicorn.

While Joe looked at the unicorn, a little man with three pullovers on came up and took the white rabbit. He held it up by its ears, and it kicked its feet at him. Then he handed it back saying, 'Flemish?'

'Dutch,' the last man said.

'Thought it was Flemish,' the little man mumbled as he turned away.

'Dutch,' the man said again.

'Funny thing,' the little man mumbled, pulling his pullovers down, 'funny thing.'

People pushed past with bags of fruit and dogs and birds in cages but none of them spoke to the man. Then a tall boy came up and stared at the white rabbit for a while.

'How much?' he asked.

'Twelve and sixpence,' the last man said. 'It's Dutch.'

'Half a bar,' the boy replied.

'Done,' said the last man and handed over the rabbit. The tall boy left, talking into the rabbit's ear. The last man pulled at the string on the unicorn as Joe came up to pat its head. The unicorn licked Joe's hand.

'What if he is a bit twisted,' the man replied, 'he'll grow straight in time.'

'He is a bit twisted,' Joe replied looking at the unicorn's hind legs, 'and one leg is shorter than the other at the back.'

'He's a runt all right,' the man said. 'Still.'

'How much is he?' Joe asked.

'Only five shillings,' the man said.

'Give you two shillings,' Joe said.

'Come orf it,' the man said.

'He's a bit twisted,' Joe said.

'What if he is a bit twisted,' the man replied, 'he'll grow.'

'Give you two and fourpence,' Joe said.

'Kids,' the man said, 'Kids.' He turned into the arches, the unicorn limping beside him, and Joe behind them both.

Under the arches the air smelt of smoke and horses, and footsteps and voices echoed through the smell. In the corners old men with long beards and old women with feathers stuck in their hats, all wrapped up in rags, sat on sacks talking to themselves. As Joe passed, an old man took a long draught from a bottle, and coughed. At the other end of the arches the last man began to hurry, and the unicorn tripped and skipped after him.

When Joe caught up with him the man stopped and the unicorn sat down.

'You still 'ere?' the man asked. 'Kids.'

'What will you do with him?' Joe said.

'Have him for dinner,' the man said.

'Oh,' Joe gasped.

'With a few onions,' the man said.

'How much is he?' Joe asked.

'How many more times?' the man said. 'Five shillings. He cost me that to raise.'

'If you come back with me to Mr Kandinsky at Fashion Street,' Joe said, 'he'll give you five shillings.'

'All that way?'

'And I'll give you two and fourpence as well,' Joe added.

'Give me the two and fourpence then,' the man said and Joe counted the coins into his hand.

'I don't mind leading him,' Joe said, 'if you're a bit tired.'

Back at the workshop Mr Kandinsky was fixing the zip

fastener into the trousers because, after all, the customer is always right, even when he's wrong. He was talking to the baker from the corner. 'You know,' he was saying, as Joe came in leading the unicorn, 'the black bread agrees with me better, only I get the heartburn something terrible.'

'I'm telling you,' the baker said, 'it's the black bread. I'm a baker, shouldn't I know?'

'Hello, Joe,' Mr Kandinsky said, 'what you got there?'

'Cripple, ain't it?' said the baker.

'It'll grow,' the man said.

'Can you lend me five shillings to pay for this unicorn, Mr Kandinsky?' Joe said.

'For a unicorn,' said Mr Kandinsky, reaching for the box he kept his change in, 'five shillings is *tukke* cheap.'

Later, Mr Kandinsky made a careful examination.

'Clearly,' he said, 'this unicorn is without doubt a unicorn, Joe; unmistakably it is a genuine unicorn, Shmule. It has only one small horn budding on its head.'

'Let's see,' said Shmule. Then after he looked and felt the horn bud he said, 'Granted only one horn.'

'Second and still important,' continued Mr Kandinsky, 'Joe went to the market to buy a unicorn. That is so, Joe?'

Joe nodded.

'Consequently,' Mr Kandinsky continued excitedly, 'it follows that he wouldn't buy something that wasn't a unicorn. In which case, he bought a unicorn, which is what this is.'

'There's a lot in what you say,' replied Shmule, 'although it looks like a baby goat, a little bit crippled that's all, not like a horse which is, after all, a unicorn except for the horn.'

'And this has a horn, yes or no?' asked Mr Kandinsky.

'Definitely,' replied Shmule, 'it has an undeveloped horn.'

'One horn only?' asked Mr Kandinsky.

'One horn,' agreed Shmule.

'So,' concluded Mr Kandinsky, 'it's not a unicorn?'

'What do I know?' said Shmule shrugging his shoulders. The shrug reminded him of his shoulder muscles, so he went on flexing and unflexing them for a while.

Then Mr Kandinsky sent Joe to the greengrocery to buy a cabbage and some carrots. 'And a couple of heads of lettuce as well,' he added. 'What he don't eat, we can put in the stew.'

While Joe was gone, Mr Kandinsky examined the unicorn again, while Shmule practised a half-Nelson on himself.

As he ran his hand over the unicorn, Mr Kandinsky sang:

One kid, one kid, which my father bought for two farthings.

Shmule looked around. 'That's what I say,' he said. 'A kid.'

'What harm will it do, Shmule,' asked Mr Kandinsky, 'if we make it a unicorn? Oy,' he added, 'he really is crippled.' Sadly beating his fist on the bench Mr Kandinsky sang:

> *Then came the Holy One, blessed be He,*
> *The angel of death to destroy utterly*
> *That struck down the butcher*
> *That slew the ox*
> *That drank the water*
> *That quenched the fire*
> *That burnt the stick*
> *That beat the dog*
> *That bit the cat*
> *That ate the kid.*

Shmule's low voice joined Mr Kandinsky's cracked one in the chorus. Together they finished the song.

One kid, one kid, which my father bought for two farthings.

THREE

ALL the excitement about the unicorn was one thing, but Shmule had his own troubles. Second, there was the dreaded Python Macklin, but first there was Sonia.

Sonia was the daughter of Hoffman the butcher, and maybe plenty of meat was the reason why she was the strongest girl between Bow Church and the Aldgate Pump. She was four inches taller than Shmule, and she had only three muscles less than him, and those muscles anyway it didn't suit a girl to have. She could lift Shmule as easily as he could lift Joe, and though she had squinty eyes and a bad temper, she had a very good figure. One day, Mrs Levenson, the corsetière, who did a bit of match-making on the side, got him over to Hoffman's for Friday night supper, and in no time Shmule found himself engaged to Hoffman's daughter Sonia. That was his number one trouble, for although a promise is all very well in its way, what is the use of being engaged if you haven't got a ring to prove it? And Sonia hadn't a ring.

That ring. Sonia didn't forget it for a minute. In the evenings or at week-ends when they practised weight-lifting together and catch-as-catch-can, she never forgot. Shmule might say, 'I pulled a muscle' – that's all. Just 'I pulled a muscle.'

'You got a muscle?' Sonia would ask, insinuating.

'Don't worry about me,' Shmule would tell her, 'I got enough muscles.'

'I forget,' Sonia would answer, lifting up the heavy bar, 'it's diamonds you are a bit short of just now.' Always on for a ring.

Do Sonia justice, the other girls in the blouse factory where she worked wouldn't let her forget. Every day one or other of them tried to needle her about the ring. 'Funny thing,' Dora the blonde – blonde!—said, 'funny thing a fellow proposes but no ring. You sure, Sonia, he said *marry*?' And even worse. Sometimes girls ran up and down showing off the rings their fellows had given them, and then Sonia felt so small. But she couldn't tell Shmule all that. The only thing to do was keep at him, because,

give credit, a girl engaged is after all entitled to a ring. Say what you like, right is right.

Because of that ring Shmule went in for the wrestling. Before that, he took three pound seventeen he saved in a slate club the baker ran, and bought a gold ring with a little tiny diamond in it. Shmule went into fourteen shops until he found a ring for that money, because everyone knows nothing but diamonds is right for engagements. But he could have saved himself the trouble. He went round to Sonia that night, pleased as punch, and when they were sitting in the front room just as Sonia was about to start nagging him, he jumped up, ran round the room, and shouted, 'Say no more – you got yourself a ring.' He gave her the ring and held his face forward for a kiss.

Who can satisfy women? A fine kiss that Sonia gave him. With the back of her hand she gave him a slap on the cheek and burst out crying.

'Two years I've waited you should make me respectable with a ring, and what do you give me in the end? A little tiny bit of rubbish, I wouldn't be seen dead in it. Why did I ever say yes to you? Why am I such a fool? Why did I let you take me to Epping Forest that time?' Because that was something else she never let Shmule forget, although there had been no trouble.

To cut a long story short, Shmule explained to Mr Kandinsky, Sonia couldn't wear that ring because such a small diamond after such a long time would make her look ridiculous. The other girls might say, insinuating, 'For such a small ring you must wait two years?' And that was why, answering Mr Kandinsky's question, 'Why be a wrestler?' Shmule took up wrestling. Wrestling he could win enough money to buy Sonia a large ring, and then perhaps, she would stop nagging him.

'Why don't you just marry the girl straightaway, and save yourself trouble?' Mr Kandinsky asked. 'Surely this is a practical solution?'

'You think I haven't tried?' said Shmule. 'She won't let me come near her until she gets that ring.'

'Why don't you marry someone who's got a ring already?' asked Joe.

'What can you know about these things?' asked Shmule.

'My mother hasn't got a diamond ring,' Joe said.

'Do me a favour,' Shmule replied, dismissing the whole matter. 'I got enough worries. This dreaded Python Macklin I got to fight soon is no joke.'

But although Shmule had worries of his own, he helped Joe to build a house for the unicorn. They got four orange boxes and a hammer and some nails, and while Shmule knocked them together he told Joe what he would do if he didn't have to develop his muscles to fight the dreaded Python Macklin. Because wrestling kills you for perfect efficiency, Shmule said. Take Fred Hercules, for instance, no use as a wrestler at all, but still the best developed man in the world. And if you could win a title like Mr World, or Mr Universe, or just plain Mr Europe, you were made. That's what Shmule might have been if he didn't ruin himself becoming a good wrestler. Mr Universe. That was something to be. Mr World. You could sign adverts; I grew my muscles on Brymaweet, signed Shmule. I always use a Rolls-Royce car, signed Shmule. It was a gold-mine, and he had to give it up. 'Turn all that in, my future, Hollywood even, because plenty of Mr Worlds have finished up big stars, just because Hoffman's daughter Sonia must have a bigger ring than any other machinist in Gay-day Blouses.' And Shmule gave one of the orange boxes such a bang with the hammer the side caved in and they had to repair it before going on.

After the house was finished, while Shmule filled up a few cracks in it with canvas, Joe went back into the workshop.

'So, how is the unicorn's house coming along, Joe?' asked Mr Kandinsky, peering through the steam from pressing, and wrinkling his nose, because after all these years he still didn't like the smell.

'Shmule is worried about that Sonia,' answered Joe. 'She wants him to turn in his future, and not have a Rolls-Royce car.'

'Women,' said Mr Kandinsky. 'But we can't do without 'em.'

'You do,' said Joe.

'I'm old, replied Mr Kandinsky. 'I have had my share of trouble.'

'Did you want to be Mr World, Mr Kandinsky?' asked Joe.

'Mr Kandinsky is already enough for Mr Kandinsky,' said Mr Kandinsky, pressing hard with his iron and making a great cloud of steam. 'The only thing I could do with, because all this bending over ironing gives me a creak in my back, is a Superheat Patent Steam Presser.' Mr Kandinsky leaned back from the bench. 'You know, Joe, with this patent steam presser all you got to do is open it – so. You put in your trousers – so. Close it – so. Press a handle. Pouf. Up comes the steam. Open. There is your trousers pressed. No smell, no consumption. Not like this, hot up the irons, press a bit, they get cold, wet the cloth, press a bit more, hot up the iron again, breaking your back, your heart, day after day.'

Whenever he thought of it, Mr Kandinsky ran on about the Superheat Steam Presser. Once he took Joe to see one working at a factory in Commercial Road. They watched a boy open and close it while another boy put the trousers in and took them out, and Mr Kandinsky looked sad when they left.

'If a man has to be a trousers-maker,' he said, 'it's a pity he shouldn't have a Superheat Steam Presser.' On the way home he took Joe into a restaurant and they had sweet lemon tea and biscuits.

Usually when Mr Kandinsky mentioned how he would like a patent presser, Joe spent some time suggesting ways for them to save up for one. But now all he said was, 'Maybe my father will send you one from Africa for your birthday,' because his mind was too busy thinking about the unicorn.

Until the unicorn's own house was finished, he lived in the workshop under a shelf, in a nest made up from odd pieces of material. Joe fed him morning and evening, leaving a bowl of water and milk for him to drink should he feel so inclined. Joe talked to the unicorn between meals so that he shouldn't feel lonely, but though he would make quite a good breakfast, he didn't care much about anything.

He just looked at Joe with sad eyes and slowly folded another lettuce leaf into his mouth with a long pink tongue.

'I think,' Joe told Mr Kandinsky, 'that this unicorn is missing his mother and father, but what can you do?'

'What can you do?' agreed Mr Kandinsky.

'But where are they?' asked Joe.

'In Africa, no doubt,' said Mr Kandinsky.

'But how did the baby get here?' asked Joe.

'Who can say? Maybe he was left here when the unicorns left.'

'But by now he should be grown up,' Joe said after a while, Mr Kandinsky put down his iron.

'There, Joe,' he said, 'you have a problem. That unicorn should be grown up.'

'But he's not,' Joe said, 'he's no bigger than a dog, not a big dog either.'

Mr Kandinsksy thought for a while.

'He is not grown up,' he said at last, 'and you know why? Because unicorns can't grow up on their own. They have to be told how by grown-up unicorns. Same as you have to be told by me, otherwise how will you grow up? Same thing with unicorns, which are, after all, only human.'

He took up his iron again, turned the flat of it towards his face, and spat lightly on it. There was no fizz. 'These blankety irons,' he said. 'What I need is a Superheat Patent Presser.'

That evening when Joe's mother came home from work, she asked first and foremost how the unicorn was. Joe said the house was nearly finished, but the unicorn didn't seem to care, and he told her what Mr Kandinsky said about why the unicorn happened to be there at all.

'Mr Kandinsky knows,' Joe's mother said, 'because he reads so many library books. I've got a surprise for you, Joe.' She brought out a bar of *halva*, a sweet made from honey and nuts wrapped in thick silver paper.

After his supper, Joe ate a piece of *halva*. He broke it

into very small bits, arranged them on the table, and ate them one at a time. He was thinking and he thought better this way.

When Joe was in bed his mother kissed him and said good night, and was about to leave when he sat up.

'You know,' Joe said, 'Mr Kandinsky wants a Superheat Patent Presser, and Shmule wants to be Mr World, and Sonia, that's Shmule's girl, wants the biggest ring in Gay-day Blouses, and that unicorn wants its mother and father.'

'And what do you want?' Joe's mother asked.

'I'm thinking what,' Joe said. 'What do you want?'

'Whatever you want,' Joe's mother answered. Then she said good night again; the whole thing all over again; a cuddle with kisses, a cuddle without kisses, one big kiss, an a few little kisses as she had done since he was young.

FOUR

THEY called the unicorn Africana, because Mr Kandinsky said that was the name for everything to do with Africa. Straightaway the unicorn began to look a little better. Everybody needs a name, otherwise how can they know who they are? You couldn't call a unicorn Charlie or Hymie, or Kandinsky even, so they called him Africana.

Every morning when he had finished his breakfast, Joe took Africana for a walk up Fashion Street, then across the road and back again past the shirt factory. Africana wore a tartan lead and collar which had belonged to the baker's dog Nicolai, named after the Tsar of Russia, both of whom were dead. The shirt factory was dead, too. It was set back a little from the road, and the whole of the front was covered with torn posters. The big door of the factory was painted a sort of purple which flaked off all the time, and had initials carved on it by the boys in the street. Above the height to which the boys could reach was still part of a large coloured poster which showed a magician in a top hat taking a blue rabbit, two blue pigeons and a large bunch of blue flowers out of another top hat. The roof of the shirt factory had small roofs on it and Mr Kandinsky called it the Kremlin. Beside the door there was a faded board which still said, 'Wanted: Machinists,' but no one ever went into the factory and the door had a large iron padlock chained on to it.

The two corners where the pavement curved round to meet the far walls of the factory were sheltered from the wind. In one or other of them there often sat one or other of the old men and women who wandered about the East End wrapped up in rags and carrying sacks, with feathers in their hats and crusts of bread sticking out of their pockets.

They only talked to themselves, mumbling all the time, sometimes having arguments alone, and once in a while shouting out so that crumbs of bread flew from their tooth-less mouths. They were wanderers, wandering through the small back streets, poking into dustbins and hiding empty bottles and rags in their sacks, begging stale loaves from the baker shops, and sleeping under the arches or in the sheltered corners of the shirt factory. No one knew them, or where they came from, or where they went. They had always been there. They were very old.

On Africana's morning walks Joe introduced him to the neighbours. Their first call was the baker, who gave them a coconut biscuit each and remarked on how Africana was growing.

'Do you really think he's growing?' Joe asked, because it seemed to him that Africana was no bigger than before.

'Growing?' said the baker, 'I should say so. And he's walking better into the bargain. Fashion Street agrees with him. You want another biscuit?'

'No thank you,' Joe replied. But Africana said nothing. He didn't even finish his biscuit.

Whenever it wasn't raining, even in the winter, Mrs Abramowitz, who had a small fancy button shop, used to sit by the open door on a bentwood chair watching people pass. Joe knew that Mrs Abramowitz meant no harm, but he wished she wouldn't pinch his cheek like a hen's bottom, because it made him feel as if he was going to be cooked, and also it hurt. Whenever she called out, 'So, my Joe, how is your Mummy?' so that Joe would have to stop and talk to her, he tried to keep his cheeks out of her way. But it was difficult to talk to people without turning your cheeks towards them, and Mrs Abramowitz was very cunning. While he was busy and off his guard telling her something, a bony hand suddenly jumped up and two bony fingers caught one of his cheeks. 'What a boychick!' Mrs Abramowitz said, licking her lips as if she was tasting him. She smelt of wintergreen ointment and camphor balls, and wore a cardigan with fancy buttons on it.

Another cheek-pincher was the man with the twisted mouth who had the confectionery and tobacconist. He wore a black Homburg hat all the year round, and tried to cover his twisted mouth by growing a bushy moustache which although his hair was grey, came out red. But you could still see it was twisted. Everyone got their sweets and tobacco from him, but he was not well-liked, being as he was a fence and an informer, a friend to the police. No one trusted him because he got the street a bad name, although he was very pious and quoted Gems at you when you went to buy a bar of milk chocolate or some Polish fruit bon-bons. His favourite Gem was 'Go to the ant, thou sluggard, consider her ways and be wise,' which he said all the time to his daughter, who also had a twisted mouth, although she couldn't grow a moustache so well to hide it. To Joe he would say, 'There is a time for all things; please don't bring the animal into the shop.' Then when he took the money, 'Two and a half to make you laugh.' Joe never laughed because suddenly, if you got too near, the fingers crawling over the polished counter quick as spiders, jumped up and bit your cheek, harder than Mrs Abramowitz. But it was the only shop which sold Polish bon-bons, Mr Kandinsky's favourite, so what could you do?

The only one in Fashion Street Joe discussed Africana frankly with was Mavis from the greengrocery. Mavis had a money box in her shop for Our Dumb Friends, although she agreed with Joe that animals talk to one another. She was always helpful with hints and suggestions so Joe let her into the secret that Africana was a unicorn. He let her feel the one horn bud which was still very small, and asked her if it was rubbed with wintergreen would it grow faster. Mavis didn't think it would, but she showed Joe how to brush Africana's coat, and always saved the best left-over greens for him and didn't charge. She said she was

sorry she couldn't do anything about the limp, except ask Her Holy Mother to help. Mr Kandinsky thought it was nice of Mavis and Her Holy Mother to go to the trouble, and besides, it might do some good. The unicorn did get a bit better at walking, so thanks were due to Mavis and Her Holy Mother, although Shmule helped as well.

Shmule studied Africana carefully. One day he said to Joe, 'Remediable exercise is the thing for that limp. Oliver at the gym told me. Works wonders.' And he massaged Africana every night for a week with a little white oil. But even with Mavis and Shmule both working, you couldn't honestly say that Africana was growing much.

'Why should you worry if he grows or not, Joe?' asked

Mr Kandinsky. 'Take everything for what it is, don't try to improve it, Joe. A chicken is a chicken. A man is a man. A little unicorn is a little unicorn. It's enough.' Mr Kandinsky thought Joe expected too much sometimes.

Joe didn't answer. He could see Mr Kandinsky wasn't in the mood to talk about things. He and Shmule were finishing off a big order. They had to work overtime to make it pay, and there was hardly enough time to eat. So naturally something had to be sacrificed, and of course, it was talking, especially as Shmule had his fight coming off soon, and never talked much in a period of intensive training, not even to Sonia. Joe was very lucky then to have Africana's company. When the weather was dry they played in the yard together, Joe in a muffler and overcoat and Africana in a woollen coat Mavis knitted him.

Joe's favourite game was called Africa. In it he and Africana explored a jungle looking for a lost city. Africana was very big and strong with an enormous solid ivory horn with silver bells on it. Joe was tall and very brown and carried a rifle and two pistols. He rode Africana through the jungle where they fought a lion, two tigers, a rogue elephant, a dreaded python two hundred feet long, and a cannibal king who looked like one of the wanderers. They beat them all. Joe wrestled the cannibal king and caught him in the dreaded scissors grip, so that his back cracked like the chair Shmule broke that time. The cannibal king was stuffed full of bits of stale bread and rags which fell out because he had wanted to steal Africana's horn and sell it. Africana defeated the elephant, and speared one of the tigers, and Joe shot the rest. Then they stopped under a big tree for a picnic dinner, and Africana had some greens while Joe brought his meat and potatoes into the yard to eat. After dinner they went on through the jungle. It was a long trek but down by the lavatory they suddenly came upon the lost city.

In the distance it looked like the shirt factory, with hundreds of cupolas all made of gold shining in the sun. In the city, which smelt of Keatings Powder, everything shone with big diamonds. Joe put one in his pocket to take back for Shmule to give his girl Sonia. The city was empty, although everything was neat and tidy as if his mother had just cleaned through. In one of the treasure vaults they found a large brand-new Superheat Patent Steam Presser which Joe put on one side for Mr Kandinsky.

Joe and Africana walked down a long road paved with silver cobbles. All the way along were stalls with singing birds and hens and hokey-pokey ice cream and fritters and jellied eels and Polish bon-bons, and you could take whatever you wanted. At the end of the road there was a huge palace like the Roxy Cinema in Whitechapel Road, shining with coloured lights.

As they walked up to the palace there was suddenly a great thunder of hoofs, and hundreds and hundreds of unicorns came galloping towards them. At the head of them there was an enormous unicorn, his great golden horn studded with diamonds, and beside him a milk-white lady unicorn with a very kind face. Africana shouted out to them, and they ran up to him and licked him all over, because they were his father and mother. On Africana's father's back – and this was the best of all – rode Joe's own father, who lifted Joe up onto his knee.

Then Joe and his father and Africana and his mother and father packed the diamond for Shmule and the Superheat Patent Steam Presser for Mr Kandinsky, and went back through Africa with all the unicorns following them, back, back, all the way back to Fashion Street. That was how Joe brought the unicorns back from Africa where they were lost for all those years.

The afternoon Mr Kandinsky and Shmule went to deliver the rush job, it was raining, and Joe and Africana played the game called Africa in the workshop.

Joe was wrestling with a chair which was the cannibal

king. He was having a hard time because the cannibal king was becoming a better wrestler all the time because of all the practice. Joe was twisting round into a better position to put the old scissors on him, when he saw a very old torn pair of boots stuffed with rags standing near his head. He looked up. It was one of the wanderers.

The wanderer had an old cloth cap with tickets in it, a big red nose, and a dirty beard all over his face. He held a sack in his hand, and a bottle stuck out of a pocket in one of his two overcoats. His little pink misty eyes peered all round the workshop. He asked Joe, 'Is the old guvner in?' although he could see that he wasn't.

Joe knew at once who it was. He watched him carefully, clenching his fists, but when he walked over to Africana he nearly screamed. It was the cannibal king all right. Joe had no rifle and no pistols and couldn't wrestle and it was real. He stared up from the floor as the cannibal king came closer and closer to Africana.

Then, thank God, Joe heard clattering on the steps and Shmule's voice say he was wet through. He jumped to his feet and ran out of the room. 'Quick, quick,' he shouted, the tears running down his face, 'quick, quick, quick.' They rushed into the room while Joe, biting his lip, followed behind.

The wanderer looked up, squinting his misty eyes at them. 'Ow are ye, guvner?' he said. 'Got any old bits of clorth terday?'

Mr Kandinsky sighed.

'You frightened the boy,' he said. 'Shmule, give him some of the bits and pieces. It's all right, Joe,' he said, 'nothing to worry for, Joe.'

Joe didn't answer. He watched the wanderer fill up his sack. All the time he looked secretly at Africana, with a look like Mrs Abramowitz when she was giving a pinch.

When the wanderer went, Joe saw him stop on the steps. Before turning out into the driving rain he pulled the bottle from his pocket and took a long drink from it. Afterwards, Joe went slowly up the stairs and looked out into the street. The cannibal king was stumbling against the wind, the sack over his back. There was a smell of methylated spirit in the passageway.

FIVE

AFTER the cannibal king tried to steal Africana, Joe was more careful. Before putting Africana's collar and lead on for the morning walk, he went out into the street to see if it was safe. Even if it was, he no longer led Africana past the shirt factory, because you couldn't be too careful. He also decided to brush up his wrestling in case it should come to that, so it was good luck that Shmule was just then in a period of intensive training.

Shmule had already beat Louis Dalmatian, who was, to tell the truth, a push-over, and the Stepney Thrasher was off with a broken collar-bone. So Shmule's manager, Blackie Isaacs, who ran the gymnasium, thought it was a lucky opportunity for Shmule to do Turk Robert and Bully Bason on the quick, and have a go at the dreaded Python Macklin, who was anyway not in such wonderful shape, he heard, owing to his stomach ulcer proving troublesome because he couldn't leave fried food alone, not to mention the booze. It was Shmule's big chance and Blackie fixed for him to fight Turk Robert and Bully Bason in the same week – Bully on the Monday and the Turk on the Friday.

It wasn't so bad as it sounds, Blackie said, because Bully was being paid off to be disqualified in the fourth for persistent gouging. 'Supposing,' Shmule asked, 'I only lose one eye, do you take half commission?'

'Suddenly,' Blackie said aloud to himself, 'suddenly our Maccabeus has got the wind up. I'm telling you,' he told Shmule, 'the Bully is being paid off – just keep your eyes closed and scream – it's too much to ask for a five-pound purse?'

As for the Turk, he only had two tricks, a deathly rabbit punch and a back-breaking full-Nelson. 'You're up to that, kid,' Blackie told Shmule. 'I know you won't let us down by letting that deadbeat murder you.' And he gave him a good rub-down.

Though he wouldn't talk to Joe about wrestling, except to say it was a mug's game, Bully and the Turk were on Shmule's mind all the time. Between stitching he weaved his head from side to side, and as he lifted the iron he would suddenly duck. All Joe had to do was watch.

The weather was cold, so by special arrangement with Mr Kandinsky, Africana was sleeping in the workshop, and as the workshop had a double lock for insurance purposes it was safe. Joe could consequently pay more attention to the wrestling business than he could with Africana living in the yard. Someone might get into the yard by climbing over the backs of the houses, but you couldn't break in through a double lock for insurance purposes. Also Africana liked it better in the workshop because it was warm and there was nearly always company. He lay under the bench in the nest of off-cuts, looking with bright eyes from one face to another. He needed rest because he had a bit of a cold.

Mr Kandinsky was worried, which didn't make things easier. He was first of all worried about his rheumatism, which was always worse in a sharp spell. He was also worried about Shmule and all this prize-fighting. He was, into the bargain, worrying about a patent steam presser because with the work short it was getting to be more and more difficult to compete. And now there was the unicorn to worry about as well. 'He don't look so good to me, Joe,' he said. 'A little animal like that should be full of beans, jumping and skipping, not lying about the whole day with hardly appetite for a lettuce leaf unless you beg him to take it.' He bent down to Africana. 'Go on then,' he said, offering a piece of leaf, 'get it down, it'll do you good. Oy – the roimatismus is killing me. And business so bad into the bargain.'

Business was so slow that Shmule said could he spend a couple afternoons at the gymnasium, especially since he had the two fights coming off and needed all the training he could get, not that he would mind how long he worked if there was the work there, but like this even his finger muscles would be cramping up waiting for the next pair of trousers, not that he wanted to put the mockers on the business, far from it, but why should he sit here messing about making new patterns when they didn't have the work. 'Do me a favour,' said Mr Kandinsky, 'go and wrestle.'

'Can I come with you?' Joe asked, and Shmule was so pleased to be going off he said Joe could, so long as he didn't talk too much and take his mind off serious matters.

Then, after telling Joe to be quiet, Shmule didn't stop talking all the way to Blackie Isaacs in Middlesex Street, behind Isaac's fish shop which was his real business.

'You see,' Shmule said as they walked round the back streets, 'I got to think of all the angles. Take the Bully, for instance. He may take the duck in the fourth all very well, but suppose he doesn't? Also I got to think of my self-respect. If I can beat him fair, it's better, I don't care what Blackie says. So it's no good you saying don't worry because the Bully is taking a duck.'

'I didn't say don't worry,' said Joe.

'I got to keep after him whether he wants to drop out or not,' Shmule went on. 'After all, that's his business. He can be paid off if he likes, that's not my affair. If it pays him better, good luck to him, let him lose on purpose.'

'Why does it pay the Bully better to lose?' Joe asked.

'You can't tell,' Shmule said. 'Maybe his manager put money for him on me and they got good odds because the Bully is an old-stager and they thought he would wrap me up with no trouble. On the other hand, supposing he don't get thrown out for gouging, and I'm taking it easy thinking, what the hell, no need to break my neck, and the

Bully give me a welt, I'm out. No, say what you like, no matter what, I got a fight on me hands. Then there's the Turk. I seen him fight three four times. True he's only got the two grips, but never mind, you've only got the one neck, he's only got to break it the once, no more. And he's got a nice style the Turk, even if he is a bit past it. He must be turned forty.'

'So old?' Joe asked.

'At least,' Shmule said. 'At that age you haven't got the speed, well you can't expect it, can you?'

'No,' said Joe.

'But he knows a thing or two all right, all right, one or two tricks to give somebody something to think about and no answer back. I got to keep out of his way and watch out for that little opening then rush him and give him the lot. Otherwise curtains. Also I'm giving him half a stone, remember, and weight counts in the wrestling. Supposing he gets his knee into me gut, I've finished, had me lot. Just because he's got the weight. No good complaining then, is it? It's all right for Blackie. He don't have to fight 'em, but if he did he wouldn't be so pleased. Two in a week. I ask you.'

'I ask you,' Joe said, 'I ask you.'

'It's too much, Joe,' Shmule said, shaking his head as they got to Isaac's fish shop.

'I ask you,' Joe said.

In the shop they were hosing the fish down, being as it was late in the afternoon and still not sold out. Mrs Isaacs who had a great mane of red hair like a lion and a hoarse whispering voice, sprayed the hose over the floor.

'Hello, Ham,' she said to Shmule, short for Hammer. 'Hello sonny,' she said to Joe. 'Gonna wrestle him, Ham?' she said, laughing till she coughed.

'Hello, Hammer,' said Miss Isaacs, who was also red-headed, giving Shmule a friendly smile. Sonia made a scene once because she was so friendly, too friendly Sonia said, to anyone in trousers, and Shmule a trousers-maker into the bargain.

'Lo, girls,' Shmule said, 'behaving?' He hitched his shoulders.

'Going to win for me next week, Hammer?' asked Miss Isaacs, with that smile. That was what Sonia called it, that smile. Miss Isaacs looked up from under her long lashes, and her eyes were a nice green-grey, very nice with deep red hair.

'For you alone, Reen,' Shmule said.

'And is Sonia doing well with her weight-lifting then?' asked Miss Isaacs, looking down.

'Such a strong girl,' Mrs Isaacs whispered.

'Very nice,' Shmule said.

'I do admire her,' Miss Isaacs said. 'Sometimes I wish I was a bit more developed myself,' and she gave Shmule that smile again.

'This way, Joe,' Shmule said.

'That Miss Isaacs has got nice eyes,' Joe observed.

'I got no time for such things,' Shmule said.

In the gymnasium, Blackie and Oliver, the second, were putting Phil Jamaica, the coloured boy, through his paces. Blackie smoked a cigar and watched closely, grunting every time Phil Jamaica hit the bag. Oliver was a punchie and you couldn't knock him out, though if he hung one on you, you knew it. He was a porter when there was work, at Spitalfield's Fruit Market, and could carry eight baskets on his head at once. He helped out as second and would give anyone a fight for five shillings, hit him all you like. Now he was crouching by the bag, his fists following Phil's. The coloured boy was covered with sweat and his eyes stared fiercely at the bag as if it might hit back if he wasn't careful. Blackie saw Shmule come in and waved his cigar.

'All right, Phil,' he said, 'turn it in.' Oliver sat Phil down, puffing and blowing, and whispered into his ear as he rubbed him down.

'Good boy,' Blackie said, when Shmule told him he was putting in extra training, 'good boy.' Shmule went into the little changing room at the other end of the gym. 'Put 'em up,' Blackie said to Joe, squaring off to him, 'put 'em up and let's see what you're made of?'

Joe got into the proper position of defence and Blackie sized him up, still puffing at his cigar. Then Joe suddenly let go and punched Blackie all over his stomach, so that he swallowed some smoke.

'Turn it in, kid,' choked Blackie, 'I wasn't ready. See the kid?' he said to Oliver, 'a champ in the making. Save it for Phil,' he said to Joe, 'he's in training.'

'What's your name, boy?' Phil Jamaica asked Joe. His eyes were not staring now, and he had his breath back.

'Joe,' said Joe.

'Watch that old defence, boy,' Phil Jamaica said, 'you was wide open. You got to watch that old defence or you is cooked. Like this.' He squared up to the punch-bag again, shadow-boxing it like mad.

'Easy, easy, Phil,' said Oliver. 'Easy, easy, boy, don't tax yourself, Phil.' Phil whipped round and shadow-boxed in circles round him. 'Easy, easy, boy,' Oliver said.

'Was you watching the old defence, boy?' Phil asked Joe.

Joe nodded his head.

'Now you show me, boy,' Phil told him.

Joe took up the position of defence again, and jumped into action, weaving round Oliver while Phil Jamaica shouted.

'Box him, boy, box him there, boy.'

Joe was puffed afterwards.

'I watched the old defence,' he said.

'You're all right, kid,' Oliver said. 'Always lead with the right and follow with the left, one-two, one-two, like that. Don't forget, one-two, one-two.'

'One-two, one-two,' said Joe, punching hard.

'And keep up the old defence, boy,' said Phil Jamaica.

'The old defence,' said Joe.

Meanwhile Shmule limbered up. He wore crimson briefs with a white hammer in the corner, and as he lifted the weights his muscles stood up in great bands. Blackie Isaacs watched him, rubbing his hands.

'What a boy!' he said, 'What a boy, Olly, what a boy, Phil! Run a couple of rounds with him, Phil. Take Phil for a couple, Hammer,' he said.

Joe watched them wrestle for a while, but though they threw one another about, and grunted and puffed and shouted, beating the canvas, he couldn't see how it was done. First they walked round one another with their legs bowed and their arms bent. That was all right. Then suddenly one jumped onto the other, but it was usually the one who jumped first who finished up with his back on the floor grunting, while the other one twisted his leg backwards and forwards.

First one, then the other, the black man and the white man, and first a black grunt, deep and dark, then a white grunt, higher and lighter. And Oliver, the second, and Blackie Isaacs shouting first for Phil and then for Shmule, while the two of them twisted round one another on the floor.

While Joe was examining the gym, which was a big shed where they used to smoke fish in the days when it paid, and which still smelt of fish, Shmule won the bout. Joe didn't notice him winning, because he was trying to lift himself up on the horizontal bars, but his arms weren't developed enough. He knew Shmule won because Miss Isaacs was watching from the door, and suddenly there was a groan from Phil Jamaica, and a quick beating on the canvas from his hands with palms which were quite pink, and Miss Isaacs shouted out, 'Great, Hammer.'

Afterwards they had fish and chips in the frying tonight part of the shop, Blackie heaping their plates with great mountains of golden chips and fillets of plaice, all very good because the establishment used only the best frying oil.

While they ate, Blackie talked to Shmule about his two coming fights and what he had heard about how both the Bully and the Turk were finished.

'Get your scissors well up,' Blackie told him.

'And watch the old defence,' Joe told him. 'Lead with the right, one-two, one-two.'

As Joe took up the position of defence two chips dropped off his plate, one-two, on to Mrs Isaacs's clean floor.

SIX

No one expected Shmule to lose his two fights, but at the same time, to win two fights in the one week is very good and you shouldn't expect it. Consequently when Bully Bason was disqualified in the fourth round, due to persistent gouging, and Shmule went the whole length with Turk Robert to win on points after a hard fight and fairly clean, everyone was delighted.

People kept dropping into the workshop to congratulate Shmule and ask him how it felt to be a champ in the making, and what he thought his chances were against the dreaded Python, and how their money was on him. It was just as well work was a bit short, otherwise it would have been held up and that means dissatisfied customers, which is very bad for business. So that if business is bad anyway and held up, at least you aren't losing goodwill.

'Nevertheless,' said Mr Kandinsky, 'with the best goodwill in the world, a patent presser can still be a help, because in the long run people want good work, but they want it cheap as well, and how can handwork be so cheap?'

Business all over the East End was, as a matter of fact, a bit slow, and Joe's mother got a couple of days off, not that it was a holiday. She was piece-working at the milliner's and consequently didn't get paid if there was no work. But Madame Rita, her boss, a big fat man with very fine fingers, swore that it was often like that just before the spring started and the weather was after all, extra cold for the time of the year. Without sunshine to wear them in, who wanted hats? All the rain and sleet would ruin a good hat, and in bad weather who anyway would be bothered to notice whether a customer wore a new hat or not?

Joe's mother had plenty to do at home. She ran herself up a dress on Mr Kandinsky's machine, a green dress with a small red flower in it, and she made Joe three shirts and a linen jacket for the summer, if it ever came. The net result of all this being that Joe was at a loose end, because women don't talk much when they are making things, and there were so many people in and out of the workshop to talk to Shmule and Mr Kandinsky about the wrestling, that he couldn't get a word in. As for Africana, except for his bit of a sniffle, which was only seasonable since most people were coughing and hawking and sniffing and sneezing, he was all right, although he still didn't want to play about much. Joe could play the Africa game silently, but it wasn't so real indoors, especially if you had to be quiet, and you did have to with so many people about.

Though Joe kept a careful look-out, there was no sign of the cannibal king. His spies must have told him that Joe was learning a trick or two, and knowing what was good for him, he kept away from Fashion Street. But you could never tell when he might strike, so Joe mounted guard three times a day at the doorway, well muffled up against the cold weather for the time of the year.

As it turned out it was just as well, because on the Tuesday he was sucking a bon-bon and thinking that he might as well go down and at least listen to other people talking, when he saw the cannibal king turn into the street.

Joe pressed himself against the wall of the passage and waited. Sure enough the cannibal king stopped when he got to the workshop, bending down to look into the window below the grating. He watched quietly for a moment. Then he stood up, took his nose between his fingers and blew it. Then he took a piece of paper out of his pocket and studied it for a while. Afterwards he folded the paper up carefully, took a last look through the grating, and walked on.

Joe watched him the whole time. That piece of paper

was his plan for stealing Africana and the only thing to do was to follow him, find his lair, and tell the sweetshop man, the informer, who would then tell the police. As it was only cold and not raining, Joe waited until the cannibal king was a bit ahead, and followed.

All the way along, Joe watched the cannibal king carefully, ready to take up the position of defence at a moment's notice. But the old man didn't look back once, which showed how cunning he was, trying to make Joe think that he didn't know he was being followed.

Once he sat down on the kerb for a short rest, and Joe turned to look into the window of a magazine shop where there were thousands of covers in full colour. They showed horrible monsters about to eat beautiful ladies with torn dresses, and rockets going to Mars, the red planet of mystery, and boxers beating one another bloody, and cowboys shooting and gangsters shooting and Huns shooting. Joe was thinking that the pictures were exciting but not very real because you never saw things like that in Fashion Street. He started to think then how it would be if when he got back to Fashion Street a whole lot of horrible monsters were trying to get into the greengrocer's shop to eat Mavis, and her overalls were torn. When he looked round, the cannibal king was gone, which again went to show how cunning he was.

There was a little sunshine now, not much warmth in it, but it made things look brighter, especially the small pools of ice in the gutters. After looking round for the cannibal king for a while, Joe began to carefully break the ice with his heel.

Joe had just found a small pool which was solid ice safe for skating on with the toe of one foot, when there was a great clanging of bells. A fire engine rushed past, covered with ladders, hoses and firemen in helmets, the brass everywhere gleaming in the cold sunlight, the engine bright red and glossy as it flashed past. In case the fire was nearby,

Joe ran off in the direction the fire engine had taken.

Joe ran a long way keeping a sharp look-out for fires everywhere, but it was no good. The fire engine had disappeared. It's always the way with fires. You never see them, because they're tucked away somewhere you never dream could catch fire, like the one just round the corner that time when some curtains caught alight. Joe heard the bells and ran all over the place, but when he finally went round the corner, there was the engine with all the firemen standing about, and a lot of people watching, but of course the fire was out.

Joe sighed. He could tell from the way his stomach felt, that it was dinner time, and since the old cannibal was nowhere to be seen, he might just as well go home. He would have gone straight home, except that he noticed the big chocolate advert over the railway bridge and being so near, he thought he might as well have a look at Itchy Park to see if any flowers were coming up yet.

Itchy Park was an old graveyard which, though full up, had hedges and a few big old trees. Flowers grew up round the graves which were so covered with grass that without the gravestones and monuments you would think it was a real park. There were two iron benches painted dark green for your convenience, should you happen to be tired, and in nice weather old men used to meet there to talk politics, while mothers pushed their babies in prams, and children played Release round the graves. With its white stone pillars with iron fences between them, the iron all black and green, the stone all white and black and grey patches from the rain and smoke, it was like ancient Greece. In nice weather, a pleasant place for a short outing.

At Itchy Park the sun made the white stone pillars and whitened headstones shine like alabaster, and Joe dawdled between the graves on his way to one which, last spring, was covered with crocuses. He spelt out some of the shorter words which could still be read on the stones, because even

if he didn't go to school yet, Mr Kandinsky told him, there
was no need for him to be ignorant. He stopped at the
memorial with the split angel on it to see if it had split
any more lately. It had only one wing and the tip of that
was missing, so that if it did split there wouldn't be much
of that angel left, and Itchy Park was already short of
angels because they got knocked off so easily. Fortunately,
the split angel was no worse, so Joe went over to the crocus
grave.

Some of the crocuses were shooting and striped dark
green leaves showed through the grass which was winter
thin and short. One of the crocuses was quite large but it
looked as if it would never flower and felt stone cold. In
spite of the sun, blasts of wind cut through the graveyard
like wet stone knives. It was no wonder if the flowers were

frozen stiff, and the grass thin, and the angels splitting. Standing up to breathe on his fingers, Joe saw the cannibal king.

Why he didn't see him straight away Joe couldn't imagine, because he was sitting on one of the iron benches with his sack beside him, drinking from his bottle. If Itchy Park was his lair, it was certainly a cold one, although maybe one of the graves opened secretly and the king crept into it at night. Joe knelt down again behind the headstone on the crocus grave to watch.

Between taking long drags on the bottle, the king grunted and coughed, not a short dry cough like a dog, but a large wide wet rackety cough, as if his whole chest and stomach coughed with him. The choker round his throat opened and his neck showed loose skin red and raw. There was spit all round his mouth, and his eyes ran with water. As he drank and coughed he only looked like an old man in a graveyard with a bad cold in the cold time of the year.

Joe was creeping round the back to go home, when suddenly the cannibal king gave an enormous cough which shook his whole body so that his face turned purple. While he was getting his wind back, his face turned white making his beard look dark and thick. He closed his eyes and sank back on the bench, and the open bottle, which was still in his hand, dipped over so that some of the spirit poured on to his coat.

When he got home, Joe's mother and Mr Kandinsky were full of questions about where he had been and how cold he was. Joe didn't tell them about the old cannibal king. It would have been too difficult to explain why he wasn't a cannibal or a king any more, just because of the cold.

SEVEN

THE morning the spring came, Joe woke up in a circle of sunlight with a breeze blowing softly upon his face. Lying still with his eyes wide open, he listened to his mother's breathing, like the sea in the distance, a ship going to Africa. But because it was the spring, Joe agreed it was only a dream, and jumping out of bed ran downstairs without his slippers on to see if Africana had noticed the welcome visitor.

Africana was indeed awake, and so full of beans, you would never guess he didn't enjoy the best of health. In view of the weather perhaps it wasn't surprising, because with the sun you always feel full of beans and it's a pity to go to bed because you will never sleep. With the sun up in the sky ripe and heavy like a solid gold water melon, everyone feels it will be a wonderful day, and sometimes it is.

In the yard, the stones already felt warm. The rotten wood fencing which oozed in wet weather like a crushed beetle, was dry as if washed up on a beach somewhere, near pirate treasure. A weed had grown in a minute of the night on the small patch of bare ground, which in the sunshine was earth not dirt any more. It might grow into a palm tree.

Africana, awake in his house, scratched at the walls eager to play. When Joe lifted the hook on the door he at once ran out. There wasn't time for a complete game, however, because Mr Kandinsky came into the yard in his carpet slippers and quilted dressing-gown, blinking, his eyes still creased up from sleeping. He sent Joe up at once to get dressed, and put Africana back in his house until after breakfast at least. As he ran upstairs, Joe felt his own face just below the eyes, but there were no creases. He guessed Mr Kandinsky had more skin to work with.

Joe's mother's boss, Madame Rita, was quite right, there was more work going in the millinery once the worst of the winter was over. Before the spring arrived, women, like the crocuses in Itchy Park, felt it near, and began to peep round at hats. They were already, during the short spells of sunshine, looking into the window of Madame Rita's shop and saying that it wouldn't really suit me, Sadie, it's for a younger woman, and Sadie was saying but it would, Ada, it's just your style. The next stage was, they came into Madame Rita's and tried on the hats. They tried twenty hats with the brims up, then down, then sideways, then without the trimming, then with more trimming. Madame Rita watched them, his hands on his large belly, a soft smile on his face, a small black cheroot between his teeth. As they tried one hat after another, with or without trimming, he made little soft cooing noises. 'Pardon me, lady,' he would say eventually, 'the brim up is more your style.' With a push here and a push there he made the hats suit the faces they had to sit over. In the end the ladies sometimes bought the hats.

Consequent upon there being more work in the millinery, Joe's mother was kept busier and busier at Madame Rita's, putting on more and more trimming as fashion demanded, and though this is tiring, it is just what the doctor ordered for piece-workers. But they have in consequence to hurry over breakfast. The day spring came, Joe and his mother had boiled eggs, and before she had her coat on, Joe kissed her good morning and ran down to the yard – so you can tell how he hurried if his mother hadn't even left yet, and she in such a hurry as well.

The reason why Joe was in such a hurry that morning was that in his sleep he had thought of a new game and wanted to see if it would work. One of the things about games is that unless you keep adding to them and working out new ideas, they get dull – not the games really, but you get dull in the games, and then they seem dull. And games like the game called Africa are worth keeping fresh, you must admit, so no wonder Joe didn't bother about such things as turning his egg-shell over and smashing the other side of it. Sometimes there are more important things to do in life than just playing about with egg-shells, and things like that have to give way to Africa. Anyhow, you can smash egg-shells anytime, but you don't get a new idea every night you sleep.

When Joe's mother was leaving, she looked in to Mr Kandinsky's workshop to say good morning to him and tell him that she might be late, and not to worry. Mr Kandinsky pointed to the back window and nodded. Looking out, Joe's mother saw Joe talking to Africana, and waving to someone a long way off. She thought how the back of his neck was still like a baby, delicate, with a little gentle valley down the centre, because he was, after all, almost a baby with everything yet to come. How much they had to learn, what a terrible lot they had to learn. She ran away to Madame Rita's to trim spring hats for those who had already learned what suited them.

All that morning Joe and Africana played together in the yard which, due to the dry rotten fencing, had become a ship, old wooden walls. Joe was the captain and Africana on one occasion mutinied. He ran to the other end of the yard frightened by Joe shouting out, 'Fasten your jibs and loosen your mainsails, you lousy lubbers,' which is only what captains do say. That nearly spoilt the game, but they went on, after a pause for Africana to eat a cabbage leaf. They visited the South Sea Islands, where Joe drank coconut milk, which is quite like ordinary milk. Mr Kandinsky brought it out for him in an enamel mug. They found pirate treasure just under the lavatory door, a small black pebble which, when properly cut and polished, would be a black diamond. Then at last they came to Africa and had a few adventures there, but suddenly Joe felt like a talk with Mr Kandinsky. Africana's sniffle had started again so they hurried on to the lost city, met Africana's parents and Joe's father and came home quickly. By air, as a matter of fact, the unicorns growing large wings like geese for the purpose.

The reason why Joe felt like a talk was that though it was a nice thing to have a unicorn, Africana often didn't seem very interested in playing. Sometimes he sat down in the middle of a game and just chewed, which was certainly irritating, even if he did have a cold. Joe was worried too because Africana still wasn't growing much and his horn was so tiny it couldn't even grant small wishes yet. Joe once wished on it for his mother to come home at three o'clock and take him to the pictures, and instead she came home at turned six and cried because there was no letter from his father.

Whilst locking Africana up, Joe practised talking and spitting at the same time. It was a question of holding the spit loose round the tip of your tongue which you kept between your teeth, and blowing when you spoke. With a little more time, Joe would have it perfect, but where did they get those sandwich boards from? Joe went into the workshop.

'Where do they get those sandwich boards from, Mr Kandinsky?' he asked.

'Where?' answered Mr Kandinsky. 'A question.'

'From the kingdom of heaven?' suggested Joe.

'Only the religious ones,' Mr Kandinsky said.

'From the agency near the arches,' Shmule said without looking up from a turn-up he was turning up. 'I know, because Blackie Isaacs has got six of them going round with me on them versus the dreaded Python Macklin at the Baths next Saturday night. No wonder I'm worried.'

'Shmule,' Mr Kandinsky cried, 'you never said nothing.'

'Can anyone get sandwich boards near by the arches?' asked Joe.

'You fighting the dreaded Python so soon?' Mr Kandinsky went on. 'How come you are fighting him? Him next to the champion and you a new boy in wrestling almost.'

'Look,' Shmule said, 'Python is warming up, see. He's near the crown five, six year. Already he fights the champ five times. Four times he loses, once he draws. Now he wants plenty of fights, get into form and knock off the champ, who is boozing too much anyway, quick. Afterwards, plenty exhibition bouts with big money for a couple year, and buy a pub in Wapping. So with the shortage in class wrestlers, Blackie does me a favour. Also knocking off the Turk and Bully didn't help me. I'm a gonner.'

'It's wonderful,' Mr Kandinsky said, 'to think in my workshop a future champion. Wonderful.'

'Wonderful,' Shmule replied, 'I got trouble, so by you it's wonderful. I'm a gonner I tell you.'

'What kind of spirit is this?' Mr Kandinsky asked sternly. 'A nice carry on. I'm ashamed.'

'You're ashamed. You should have the worry and you wouldn't have no time to be ashamed.' Shmule threw his needle and thread down. 'That bloody Python is going to break my bloody neck.'

'Think how proud Sonia will be of you,' Mr Kandinsky said.

'Sod Sonia, let her fight the Python and I'll be proud,' answered Shmule, and he picked up his needle and got on with his sewing.

'The sandwich boards, Joe,' said Mr Kandinsky. 'The sandwich boards is an interesting case.'

'Sod the sandwich boards,' said Joe. 'That bloody Python.'

'Go to the corner and get three rolls,' shouted Mr Kandinsky in a voice of thunder and Joe ran out. 'A fine attitude to life,' Mr. Kandinsky told Shmule, his mouth turned down at the corners, which was always a bad sign.

When Joe came back he found that Shmule and Mr Kandinsky were not on speaking terms, except for essentials like 'Pass the black thread' and 'Give me the shears.' Joe couldn't break the ice by talking about what was on his mind before he thought of the sandwich boards, because he couldn't remember what it was, so after dinner he went out and spent the afternoon helping Mavis in the shop. At least Mavis always thought it was a wonderful day. She let him serve Mrs Abramowitz with a pound of Granny Smith apples, of which she was very fond. Of course Mrs Abramowitz managed to pinch his cheek, sod her.

EIGHT

THE day before Shmule's fight with Python Macklin, the workshop was closed. Shmule was getting into top shape down at Isaacs's Gymnasium and Blackie was giving every assistance, including sending out of his own pocket a case of bad whisky to Python, because even if it would be hell for the stomach ulcers, who can resist the gift of an unknown admirer? Mr Kandinsky did have, to tell the truth, a couple of things he could have got on with, but instead he spent the morning at Shafchick's vapour bath. By permission of Madame Rita, Joe spent the morning down at the milliner's with his mother, which certainly made a change from all the bad temper and arguments in Kandinsky's workshop. Furthermore, the girls at Madame Rita's gave you sweets all the time, and had a completely different kind of conversation.

Joe's mother was the trimmer, and there was another girl called Sophie who was learning the trimming from her. There was the machinist, Mrs Kramm, who was old and had a chest, and a pretty assistant from the shop named Ruby but called Lady R. Ruby was very nice to Joe but she treated the others, even Joe's mother, a bit haughty. As soon as she went out of the workroom they talked about her.

'What a fine lady, I don't think,' said Sophie.

'Some lady, I should say, and what was she before? – a little snot-nose giving the boys eyes the whole time,' wheezed Mrs Kramm.

'She's very pretty,' Joe's mother said, picking up a small bunch of artificial cherries. 'And good at her job.'

'That you can say again,' Mrs Kramm said. 'That job she can do all right, I wouldn't wish it on my worst enemy such a job she can do so well.' She pressed the treadle of her machine so that the thread shot through the needle like lightning.

'Mrs Kramm,' Joe's mother said, looking towards Joe, 'I'm surprised at you. After all, it's only a rumour.'

'Oh no it's not, Becky,' Sophie said quickly. 'I've seen him after her behind the gown rail carrying on something terrible.'

'Sophie,' Joe's mother said, 'the child.'

'Here you are, Joe,' Sophie said, 'I've found a caramel in silver paper for you.'

'Thank you very much,' said Joe, because they were the soft kind with a nut in the middle, although he would rather have heard some more about Lady R and Madame Rita. But it was just as well Sophie stopped when she did because while he was taking the silver paper off the caramel carefully so as not to tear it, who should come in but Lady R herself.

'Becky dear,' she said to Joe's mother, 'could Joe go an errand? Would you go an errand, Joe sweetie, for Auntie Ruby, dolly?'

'Certainly he could,' Joe's mother said, though Joe didn't as a rule run errands for dollies.

'Will you, dolly?' asked Lady R, bending down and putting her face right close to his. 'For me?'

'All right,' Joe said. Lady R smelt nice at least, and she had large brown eyes and a smooth dark skin and oily black hair very smooth and curled into a bun.

'Bless you, baby,' Lady R said, and suddenly she gave Joe a fat kiss on his cheek, which though better than a pinch is still a nuisance.

The errand was to go round the corner and collect Lady R's genuine French calf handbag which was having its clip repaired. When he was coming back through the shop with the handbag, which was a sack of coal over his shoulder, he saw Madame Rita and Lady R behind the

gown rail, and what Sophie said was true. Back in the workroom his mother got out her handkerchief and licked it and rubbed off Lady R's lipstick, which meant that it had been on his face all the time and he didn't know, which proves you shouldn't go errands for dollies.

'Don't lick me,' Joe said.

'Keep still, Joe,' replied his mother.

'If you lick me clean, you should lick Madame Rita, too, because his face is even worse.'

'Oy,' wheezed Mrs Kramm, 'the cat is in the bag. What goings on. For a respectable woman it's terrible.'

After Joe had been cleaned up he went down into the cellar where there were a whole lot of old dummies, coloured crepe papers, and boxes. Although he got filthy, it did allow the women to talk about Lady R, which is all women want to do anyway. For his part he got down to a serious game of Club Row.

He was being an Indian fortune teller with a green remnant round his head, when he had a happy thought. He thought how the women wanted to talk about Lady R, and how Shmule wanted to win another fight although he had already won two, and how Mr Kandinsky still wanted a patent presser, and how his father hadn't sent for them yet.

So, Joe thought, everybody is always saying I wish, I wish, and always wanting things. And straightaway he improved being a fortune teller by having Africana with him. Africana wasn't very much bigger, but his horn was coming along nicely, just big enough for, say, five or six wishes.

Joe set out four boxes, on which he made drawings with a piece of flat chalk he kept in his pocket for emergencies. One of his mother in a hat, one of Mr Kandinsky, one of Shmule and one of everybody else, including Sonia and Mavis. Then he led Africana, the wish-maker, to each box. After what was necessary was explained to Africana, he was very glad to bend his head so that his horn touched the drawing on each box. And that was how the wishes were granted. All this took a good deal of work, so it was not until Sophie came down to the cellar to call him for dinner that the job was done.

When he went upstairs he still had the green remnant round his head. Lady R, who was eating a salt-beef sandwich, waved a pickled cucumber at him and called him the Sheik of Araby dolly. If Joe didn't find something to do in the afternoon she would spoil everything, because she was that type. It was good luck that Mr Kandinsky called in while Joe was eating his second jam sandwich.

As Mr Kandinsky had spent the whole morning at Shafchick's vapour bath in Brick Lane, he looked very pink and scrubbed, but he wasn't angry about Moishe, which was unusual. He said to Joe's mother, 'That Moishe, the capmaker, went too far today. He got cooked.' And he giggled and asked Joe if he would like to come round with him to the Tailors' Union, he had to tell them about how Moishe was cooked.

Moishe, the cap-maker, had a huge belly and was an old friend of Mr Kandinsky. They argued all the time, and always met on a Friday at Shafchick's, where they would argue their way through the hot room, then the hotter room, then the hottest room in the world, and even while they were being rubbed down by Luke, the Litvak masseur, who only used the Russian massage whether you wanted it or not. Luke carefully made up his own bundles of twigs, holding them high in the steam to pick up the heat. He gave you a rub-down like an earthquake, then shook hands and said 'Good health, Reb.' He was a big man with a huge belly, and when he and Moishe stood together you could drive a pair of cart-horses between them. They carried the argument through whilst they drank glasses of lemon tea to put the moisture back into their systems, although they had just gone to all that trouble to get it out.

Mr Kandinsky's arguments with Moishe were mostly political, like Macdonald and Baldwin, which is the best man, or was the Tsar murdered or can you call it execution, or whether the Tailors' Union should run a sick fund or was it placing temptation in the way? In Shafchick's such arguments became heated especially in the hottest room in the world, because at Shafchick's you can always rely on the heat. They say that Shafchick was a great rabbi who was so pious that Barney Barnato wanted to give him something, so being pious he said what else but a vapour bath for the whole East End, and that's what Barney gave him, and of course he became managing director and did very well, so they say, but why not since at Shafchick's you can rely on the heat, day or night. It comes gliding out of a hundred small gratings slowly until the place is like a stew pot boiling on the gas. No one bothers you, you sit in a deck chair like Bournemouth or the Crimea, play chess, drink your tea, argue, whatever your pastime happens to be. All the time you are getting the benefit of the heat. Rheumatism is melted before it can crystallise round the joints of your bones, veins become less varicose, the lumbago and all creaks in the back are eased, and you get a good rest into the bargain. And afterwards? Don't ask. You feel like an angel walking through the green fields of Brick Lane. If you wanted to, you could fly looking down upon the hills of East London, while everything is fresh about you, as in the morning of life. You smell the *baigels* leaving the bake-oven. Cart-horses make the streets smell like a farmyard, and the people about you have the faces of old friends. Everything is so good when you come from Shafchick's that once you get the habit you never regret it, even if Moishe's arguments are so ridiculous they make you a bit short-tempered. It is not a real short temper. It is a luxury to make you feel deeper the joy of having lived through yet another vapour bath.

As they walked over to the Tailors' Union, Mr Kandinsky giggled most of the time, and once or twice he stopped dead, looked down at Joe and laughed out loud.

'How that Moishe was cooked,' he giggled. 'What a hot-pot.'

The Union was in Whitechapel Road, and in the week there were not many tailors there, but on Sunday mornings they filled the room and spread out into the street, chatting in their long coats about this or that, small groups of them for a hundred yards up the Whitechapel Road. Sometimes a master-tailor would come up and say, 'Have you seen Chaim? I got three days' work for him,' and everyone would shout out, 'Where's Chaim? Here's work for him.' The Union room itself was dirty, with dusty windows on which someone had written with a finger, 'Up with,' but they couldn't decide who, so there was no name. The wooden plank floor was smeared with rubbed out cigarette ends, and the only decoration on the walls was the black and red poster which said, 'Wrestling Saturday Night,' with pictures of Shmule and Python Macklin on it. A young coat-maker who happened to be temporarily unemployed was making up a small book at a table below the poster.

At one end of the room there was a trestle table with a big brown enamel teapot stewing on it, a quart bottle of milk, and a plate of rolls and butter. Behind the trestle Mrs Middleton, the caretaker, stood, cutting rolls, pouring tea, and talking Yiddish with some old tailor who, like Mr Kandinsky, looked in to hear what was happening in the world.

At another trestle table, which had benches along both sides, two men were playing dominoes. As Mr Kandinsky and Joe came in, they finished a game, and the bones clicked as four hands smoothed them over for the next, for domino games go on for ever. Two other men drank tea from big chipped enamel mugs they carried in their overcoat pockets.

'So white gold is by you cheap stuff, rubbish?' one said.

'Who says rubbish,' the other replied, 'platinum is better, that's all.'

'Platinum is good enough for you,' said the first, 'you're sure?'

'Another cup tea, Missus,' the other said.

'You didn't pay for the first two yet,' Mrs Middleton answered.

'You short of platinum maybe?' the first said, putting sixpence on the counter.

Mrs Middleton filled the cups up with black tea, and sloshed milk on top. 'Why Mr Kandinsky,' she said, 'what a surprise.' She always told her friends that Mr Kandinsky was a real gentleman.

'Mrs Middleton, my dear,' Mr Kandinsky said, shaking hands with her, 'what a pleasure to see you. So well you look, ten years younger. How's the boy?'

'He's in the sign-writing now,' Mrs Middleton said proudly.

'A good trade,' one of the men said.

'Very artistic,' said the other.

'You know,' Mr Kandinsky said to the men, 'that boy when he was twelve could draw anything you like, a pound of apples, a couple oranges, a banana, anything.'

'Maybe he should have gone in the fruitery,' one of the men said.

'No,' replied Mr Kandinsky, 'people as well, the King, politicians.'

'Bastards,' the other man said.

'A nice cup of tea, Mr Kandinsky?' asked Mrs Middleton.

'By all means, with pleasure,' replied Mr Kandinsky, 'and a glass of milk for the boy.'

'Your grandson?' asked Mrs Middleton. 'Bless him.'

'Nearly,' Mr Kandinsky said, 'bless him.'

While they drank their tea and Joe sipped his milk, which was a little dusty, Mr Kandinsky asked the men how was business, and they said he meant where was it, it was a thing of the past, tailors were two a penny if you were throwing your money away because in a couple of months the tailors would pay you to let them work. Mr Kandinsky said it was terrible, he was feeling it bad, but what could you do? And the men agreed, what could you do?

All the time Mr Kandinsky was on edge to tell them how Moishe was cooked. He was leading up to it by saying how well he felt after a vapour bath at Shafchick's. One of the men liked vapour baths very much, but the other one thought they were bad for the system, like lemon tea, tasty but rotting to certain organs of the stomach.

'You,' the other man said, 'with a barrel organ in your stomach, you couldn't make more noise, such rubbish you talk. Vapour baths is proven by the best medical authority to be the best thing in the world for the system. Lords and ladies are paying fortunes to go to foreign parts, and why? – because they got vapour baths. And here we got in the East End one of the finest vapour baths in the world, where for practically nothing you can go and sweat first or second class all day long to your heart's content. He isn't satisfied. It's rotting the organs of his stomach, Mr Platinum here.' He spat on the floor.

'Manners,' warned Mrs Middleton.

'Anyhow,' continued Mr Kandinsky, annoyed at the interruption, 'whose telling the story? You know Moishe the cap-maker from Cable Street?'

'The one who married his son to the daughter of Silkin, the wholesale grocer?' one of them asked.

'No, no,' the other said. 'Moishe is the one with the

big ears who goes to the dogs.' One of the men playing dominoes looked up and grunted.

'You know,' he said. 'Everything you know.'

'You know better?' the man replied.

'You know,' the domino player said again.

'So play,' said his partner, who was winning.

'Anyhow,' Mr Kandinsky continued, 'Moishe comes to the baths on Fridays, and you think you can argue, but that Moishe is one to argue you out of business. Doesn't matter what you say, he knows better. Whatever it is, politics, history, business, anything, he knows better. I just come from Shafchick's and you know what happened?' Mr Kandinsky stopped to giggle again and to give the domino players a chance to look round from their game. 'He just got cooked.'

Naturally they all wanted to know what happened, so after laughing a bit more to drag it out, Mr Kandinsky told them.

He and Moishe were talking about the slump and he said that if only he had a patent steam presser he could do all right, slump or no slump, because if you could do the work fast enough, it didn't matter if you got paid less, just so long as you kept turning it over, and if you keep working you can always make a living. Also with a patent presser you could take in pressing when the trousers were slack. At once Moishe says what does Kandinsky know about economical matters, leave it to the specialists who get employed to know these things, they take years of study.

'I been studying my trade with the goose iron for enough years,' Mr Kandinsky replied. 'I know what's what.'

'Kandinsky,' said Moishe, 'that's where you make your mistake. Do you know what is a price spiral with an inflation? You don't. Do you know we are dropping off from the gold standard? You don't. Do you understand the economical problem of today? You should worry.'

'What is all this to do with making trousers for a living, if you don't mind a question?' asked Mr Kandinsky.

'That's what I mean,' replied Moishe, 'trousers-making you know, but what else?'

'And what else am I talking about? I read plenty books in my time and now also, but leave that to one side, what am I talking about except trousers-making? I am saying a patent steam presser is what I need. I don't know what is good for my business?'

But Moishe went on and on about gold prices and unemployment figures. He read the financial column of the paper very carefully every day as a hobby, and he was enjoying himself, especially as there was a shortage of cap-makers and he had plenty of work.

They went into the heavy steam room, where you can hardly breathe or see at all. But in spite of that Moishe went on talking and talking from his end of the room, lying on the marble bench with his towel under him, talking and talking. So Mr Kandinsky left him to it. 'Let him talk to himself since he's the only one who knows what he's talking about,' Mr Kandinsky thought, as he went out for a massage.

He had his massage talking with Luke the Litvak about his brother-in-law, the doctor in the children's hospital, although, funny thing, no children of his own. Afterwards he sat down quietly in a deck chair in a second class cubicle. He drank a glass of lemon tea and read the paper. Then he settled down for a little sleep.

Suddenly, just when Mr Kandinsky is dreaming he is picking cherries in an orchard at home, and though the cherries are full and ripe, there is yet blossom on the trees, which is impossible but looks wonderful and the smell, there is a shouting, and he wakes up. There, the colour of borsht and steaming like a pudding is Moishe, cursing him and saying what a thing to do, locking him in like that, and it's wonderful he's alive to tell Kandinsky what kind of a lousy dog he is.

'And what happens,' laughed Mr Kandinsky 'is this. I am so fed up with Moishe talking and talking, I slam the door of the heavy steam room, and it jams. I told him, is it my fault the door jams? It's the heavy steam from him talking so much. What's it got to do with me? You should have seen him, just like a stuffed neck he looked, stuffed with red cabbage. Luke and me laughed our heads off.'

The men laughed and said it should teach Moishe to argue the whole time, they must remember to ask him how he got cooked and how was his price spiral. Then they went back to their own arguments, which since Mr Kandinsky was there, came down to the question who would win the fight tomorrow night. They placed bets with the man who was making the book, and Mr Kandinsky said as it was a special occasion he would put a shilling on for Joe. The platinum man said to the white gold man, 'Even if he don't win, I don't want to make a crust out of that lousy Python Macklin, who is, without doubt, one of the dirtiest fighters in the ring today. Also if Shmule wins, it's good for the tailors and we should all be behind him, even if he loses.'

Joe put down the buttered roll he was eating.

'Shmule will be the winner,' he said. They all looked at him in silence for a moment.

'Put another bob on, Hymie,' said white gold.

'Out of the mouths of babes,' said Mr. Kandinsky.

Just at that moment, one of the old men stopped clicking dominoes and said to Mr. Kandinsky, 'Kandinsky, you want a patent presser? My brother-in-law, the one with the big factory.'

'Big factory,' the other old man said.

'You got a bigger factory?' the first old man asked.

'So?' asked Mr Kandinsky.

'He just got a new presser for his new factory, and he's chucking out the old one.'

'It works?' asked Mr Kandinsky.

'To look costs nothing,' the old man said.

'So I'll look,' replied Mr Kandinsky, and patted Joe's head.

Joe was very pleased, especially when you remember that Africana wasn't really with him in the cellar at Madame Rita's. It may have been the green remnant, because you can never tell where an odd bit of magic is going to turn up, so why not in the cellar of Madame Rita's. Joe thought they had better get home quickly now, because it might start to happen any minute.

The first thing Joe did when they got home was to go into the yard and thank Africana. He put his arm round his neck and kissed him gently on the head, next to his horn bud. African coughed and his head jerked up and hit Joe's jaw, making him bite his tongue.

NINE

THE following day the weather was cold again. It was going to be one of those springs which stops and starts, unable to make up its mind whether to stay or not. One moment the stone streets were pink and bright in the sunshine, and the next they were grey and dirty again, the sun sunk away somewhere behind a million chimneys on a million slate roofs. But though Saturday morning brought no quick pools of sunlight and the Kremlin, a disused shirt factory, looked blank and dead in the grey light, no one bothered, for they were all impatient for the evening. Once the evening comes, what does it matter how bright or dull the day has been? So far as the evening is concerned, all days are bright, and tomorrow can be still brighter. Hurry along tomorrow, a brighter day, and for an overture, let the evening bring great moments of life such as the spectacular fight between the Aldgate Hammer and the dreaded Python Macklin. And for the sake of tailors everywhere, let the tailor win.

Shmule gave Mr Kandinsky four seats in the second row for Joe and his mother, Sonia and himself. The fights didn't begin until half past seven, and Shmule's bout came up an hour later. Mr Kandinsky was going to get them there in good time for Shmule's fight but he would in no circumstances hear of them seeing the fights which came before.

'We are not,' said Mr Kandinsky, 'savages to go and watch the gladiators fight and to enjoy the struggles of people we don't know. Shmule is our own boy, so we must encourage him, not have a good time while other people get broken necks. If it wasn't for Shmule fighting we would never go, not in a hundred years.' And even Sonia, who enjoyed wrestling even if she didn't know the wrestlers – and she knew most of them, of course – had to wait round the house talking about her trousseau with Joe's mother until it was time to leave.

Africana was shivering. Joe tried to make him comfortable in his house, which had had so many bits and pieces tacked on to it through the winter that it looked like a wooden patchwork quilt. It was a shame that animals weren't allowed at the wrestling, because if Shmule did win it would be Africana's doing. Joe promised to tell Africana everything in the morning and anyhow Africana's cough was bad. He wouldn't take Gee's Linctus, even on cubes of sugar, and what with the break in the weather making it treacherous for bronchial complaints, it was just as well for Africana to stay at home. Joe told everybody that Africana wasn't very well. Being the first dressed, he went out to have a word with Mavis on the subject.

The street looked quite different at night. Great deeps of shadow gathered in the corners of the Kremlin, and the small shops were warm with lamps. The baker's lamp was gas and spluttered, but Mavis's were electric and steady. On the street corner there was a barrow with a big naphtha lamp spitting away white and blue, and two large iron braziers with iron trays red hot on them, roasting chestnuts and baking potatoes. Someone stood by the barrow and Joe was surprised to find it was the man who helped the Eel King on Sundays, so it looked as if with the coming of the night everyone became someone else. Even Mavis looked different, older and paler in the yellow light, with tired markings on her face, her flowered overalls dirty from where she had clasped bins of potatoes all day long. She was surprised to see Joe up and about at that time of night.

'You do look a toff, Joe,' she said, 'in long trousers and a jacket to match, a real toff. Where are you off to? You should be in bed.'

'Yes they are nice,' Joe said, putting his hands deep into the pockets of his long trousers. 'They have real flies, with buttons.'

'I suppose old Mr Kandinsky run them up for you,' Mavis said. 'He run up all my old dad's.'

'You look a bit old, Mavis,' Joe said. 'The whole street looks sort of different at night.'

'I am a bit old, dear, I reckon,' said Mavis, 'and with the end of the day you feel it more.'

'You'll have to hurry because we're going soon,' Joe said, and told her about Shmule's fight.

'I shan't come, Joe dear,' Mavis said, 'there's still a lot to do though no morning market to think about, and I don't think blood sports should be allowed anyway, and wrestling is a sort of blood sport. Would you like a nice apple?'

'Thank you,' said Joe, taking a large bite of the russet apple she handed him. 'What's a blood sport?'

'Where they hunt poor dumb animals,' Mavis said, 'for their sport, like the early Christian martyrs and saints that were thrown to the lions.'

'You mean the lions ate them up?' Joe asked, thinking it was a good thing he never did get that lion cub for a pet.

'Yes, poor souls, limb from limb,' said Mavis, sorting through the tomatoes.

'They must have been hungry,' Joe said, taking another large bite of his apple.

'It wasn't them, poor dumb beasts, it was the sinfulness of their masters, and yet, Joe, they prayed for their torturers in the midst of their torment.'

'What's torturers and torment?' Joe asked, although he really wanted to talk about Africana.

'Don't trouble your head about it,' Mavis said. 'Oh, what a rotten one,' she added throwing a soft tomato into a box, where it burst juicily. 'How's your little unicorn?'

'That's what I was going to tell you,' Joe said. 'He's got

this bad cold on the chest and coughs all the time, and he's not interested in anything, and won't touch the Gee's Linctus, even on cubes of sugar. Do you think it's the consumption?' Mavis stopped sorting for a moment.

'He never was very strong you know, Joe. He was always a delicate little thing. This has been a rotten winter for the best of us.'

'I know,' said Joe, 'Mr Kandinsky has been getting terrible creaks down his back this winter, and I saw someone with a cough.' He was going to tell her about the cannibal king that time in Itchy Park, but he didn't want to think about it. 'Will you have a look at Africana, Mavis?' he said instead.

Mavis closed the shop and they walked down to the house. They went through to the yard, and Mavis wrapped Africana in a piece of blanket and brought him into the workroom. In the light from the naked bulb over Mr Kandinsky's bench Africana looked pinched and sick, and

Mavis's face was serious. While she examined Africana, Joe heard Mr Kandinsky call from the other room and went to see him.

Mr Kandinsky was walking about in polished boots, wearing a combination woollen vest and long pants.

'I can't find them blankety trousers,' he said. 'Can you imagine, Joe,' he added, 'a trousers-maker without a pair of trousers to his back. Here they are.' Grunting he drew a pair of striped black trousers out from beneath the mattress and pulled them on.

Joe told him that Mavis was in the workroom having a look at Africana who wasn't at all well. Joe made his face serious like Mavis, the lips pressed tight together.

'That animal,' Mr Kandinsky said, 'has he ever been not sick?'

'Maybe we should send him back to Africa, to his mother and father,' Joe said.

'Africa?' asked Mr Kandinsky. 'What's with Africa?'

'To the other unicorns,' Joe said, a bit annoyed because Mr Kandinsky wasn't thinking.

'Oh my God, yes,' said Mr Kandinsky. 'Africa. Maybe we should. Quite right. Have a wine cherry, but only one.' Mr Kandinsky's bedroom was almost filled by a big mahogany bed with two large feather beds on it. A huge wardrobe stuffed with clothes and books and remnants took up one wall. The other wall had a small fireplace choked with coloured crepe paper. But in the corner was a small barrel in which Mr Kandinsky made cherry wine. It was the best thing in the room, with a little tap and a mug hanging from it, full of soaked black cherries scooped from the bottom of the barrel, making the room smell always of cherries and wine. Joe took a cherry and put it into his mouth. He tasted the wine while the cherry was still on his lips. Then he bit through to the stone slowly so that the wine taste spread right through his mouth.

'So,' said Mr Kandinsky, 'I'm ready. Just let me put on

my watch. This was my father's own watch and chain, Joe. A real watch, with an albert. So, lead on Macduff. Forward to the big fight.'

In the workroom, Mavis was rubbing Africana's chest slowly, and talking to him in a whisper.

'Mavis,' said Mr Kandinsky, 'nice to see you. You coming to the fight?'

'This animal isn't at all well, Mr Kandinsky,' said Mavis. She looked in Joe's direction, and moved her head.

'Joe,' said Mr Kandinsky, 'you can take one more cherry yourself and take some upstairs for your mother and Sonia.'

When Joe had left, Mavis said to Mr Kandinsky, 'This poor little soul's in torment.'

'Oy,' said Mr Kandinsky.

'It's cruel to leave him,' said Mavis, and she was suddenly very hard and determined. 'It's cruel.'

'What must be, must be,' said Mr Kandinsky. 'But wait till we go.'

'That man should never have sold it to him in the first place. How could it live in Fashion Street?' She stroked the little animal's head just where its stunted horn buds grew so close together as to seem one horn. 'Poor little kid,' she said. 'I'll take it to the People's Dispensary.'

'You're right,' said Mr Kandinsky with a sigh. 'How can a kid like this grow up in Fashion Street? It's not strong enough. I'll find something to tell the boy.'

Joe's mother and Sonia came down the stairs, still talking about Sonia's trousseau. She had a nightdress of pure silk and another one with Flemish lace neck and hem, a shame to wear them really, except in hospital.

Joe said good night to Mavis who held Africana shivering in the blanket. Mavis would look after him, and he was pleased to go into the dark street again. He hurried ahead of Mr Kandinsky and the women, and only for one moment did he want to run back again to Africana.

'*One kid,*' sang Mr Kandinsky quietly, '*which my father*

bought for two farthings. Good night, Reb Mendel,' he said to Reb Mendel Gramophone, who stood, a little bearded shadow, at the end of the street.

Reb Mendel's gramophone on top of an old pram pushed its big cracked horn towards Joe, and sang in a fast high voice like tin, '*Eli, Eli, lamah azavtani.*'

TEN

In the Whitechapel Road it was all bright lights and crowds of people, smart as paint, taking a Saturday night stroll after working the week as machinists and under-pressers and cabinet-makers.

They queued at the Roxy for the second house, two big pictures, while an acrobat turned somersaults in the road for pennies, and sang *Any old iron*, jangling a string of real medals. They crowded into restaurants for lemon tea, and swelled out of the public houses waving bottles, their arms about each other's necks, their children waiting at the doors with glasses of lemonade clasped to their narrow chests. They walked slowly along, bright ties and high-heeled patent leather shoes, eating chips out of newspaper, careful not to let the vinegar spill onto their new clothes. Arm in arm they walked, in trilby hats, brims down, girl-friends with bright lips and dark eyes and loud laughter, mothers and fathers arguing together, calling to children licking toffee apples and taking no notice, old men talking quietly raising their eyebrows, knowing the truth of things.

Joe strode ahead of his mother, who chatted with Mr Kandinsky, while Sonia dawdled talking to a girl with heavy pencilled eyebrows and glossy silk stockings, out with her new fiancé, a bookie's runner and flash with wide padded shoulders to his blue double-breasted suit. Joe took giant strides past Russian Peter with his crooked beard and Russian peaked cap. Russian Peter usually had wreaths of garlic cloves and pyramids of home-pickled cucumbers on his barrow, a large box with handles mounted on two wheels, but now he had a tray with packets of sweets and chewing gum and toffee apples. Instead of calling out, 'Cumber, knobbel, cumber, knobbel,' as he usually did, he said, 'Taffee eppls, taffee eppls,' in the same high voice. Russian Peter's cucumbers were pickled by a special recipe he brought with him from Russia, with his peaked cap. Joe went back to ask his mother for a toffee apple. Sure enough, it had a special taste, strange, black glistening treacle.

They allowed plenty of time for the walk to the baths, which was just as well, because what with Sonia saying hello to all her friends and their new fiancés, and Mr Kandinsky talking to this one and that, and different people asking Joe's mother how was his father, they would be lucky to get there at all. As it was, when they arrived at the baths, Joe heard a great roar from inside, and thought, that's it, that's the end of the fight, we've missed it. But they hadn't. It was still the last round of the fight before.

For the wrestling season, the swimming baths were boarded over, a relief to Joe who had been wondering how they could wrestle in baths. There were big lights over a ring in the middle, and you could make out the diving boards at one end, dim in the darkness, with canvas sheets hanging over them. There was no water beneath the boards though, because Joe dropped a small stone through them and there was no splash. It was like the railings over the pavements in the streets. If you made up your mind they were fixed, it was all right. People sat in rows, on seats in front and benches behind, while further back still they stood on wide steps, sitting on the floor in the intervals.

Men went round with trays, selling hokey-pokey ice creams, roasted peanuts, and cold drinks, and there was a great hum of noise, which, during the fights, quietened down so that only one or two voices would be heard over the grunting of the wrestlers. Two wrestlers were tied up together on the floor of the ring, one of them grunting as he pressed down harder and harder, the other shouting out 'Oh, oh, oh, oh!' every time he was pressed. He wore a red mask but he was losing all the same.

Someone called out 'Wheel 'em out,' and someone else

shouted 'Carve-up,' and a red-headed woman screamed 'Tear his arms off, Mask.' All around people munched peanuts and drank ice-cold drinks out of bottles. As Joe sat down a man in a big coat started to eat a sandwich and a pickled yellow cucumber at once. At the end of the row where they were sitting, Joe saw Madame Rita and Lady R. Madame Rita had his arm round Lady R. He shouted 'Chuck 'em out, they're empty,' waving a cigar in his other hand. Lady R watched the wrestlers closely. Her eyes stared and her lips moved in a small tight smile, and when one threw the other, she clasped her hands together, breathing out hard between her teeth. Then, when they finished, she sank back in her seat and looked round with shining eyes at Madame Rita, who squeezed her shoulder in case she was frightened.

The end of the fight came while Mr Kandinsky was buying them roasted peanuts. The bell rang, and one of the wrestlers, puffing and blowing, had his arm held up by the referee, while the other one still writhed on the floor. Half the people cheered, and the other half booed. The two wrestlers, left the ring, sweating hard, their dressing gowns draped over their shoulders. One of them tripped on the ropes.

There was a good echo in the baths, although with all the shouting and laughing it was difficult to hear it, but sometimes there was a gap in the noise, people were suddenly quiet, as if getting their wind, and then one voice would ring out and the echo pick the words up and throw them back into the smoke and the smell of ozone. Joe would have liked to shout for the echo, but while it was all right under the arches, you didn't like to in front of so many people, and anyhow as soon as you decided to try it, the noise started again. 'Wheel 'em in,' they shouted. 'Money back, get on with it.' But nothing happened because it was the interval.

At the ends of the aisles St John's men in uniforms with

polished peaks and white bands sat looking out for people to faint, but no one did. Programme sellers went up and down, shouting out that the lucky programme number got two ringsides for next week. Madame Rita had two but bought two more, just to show off. The hokey-pokey men in white jackets did very well, and almost everyone was sucking orange and pink ice creams or drinking from bottles or eating peanuts, crunching the shells under their feet.

Then, just as the crowd was getting bored with lucky programmes and hokey-pokey, and restless for the big fight to start, the M.C. climbed into the ring. There was a great roar, and though he held up his arms, it went on. He shook his arms, turning from one side to the other, and the dickie front of his evening suit opened a little. 'Ladees and gentlemen!' he shouted, 'your attention if you please, ladees, your attention gentlemen, please.'

The crowd quietened and the M.C. smiled. 'For your entertainment, at great expense, Sam Spindler the well-known harmonist, will entertain you.' There was a groan as Sam Spindler, a thin bald-headed man in a Russian silk blouse with red ruching, and black trousers cut wide at the bottom but tight in the waist, climbed through the ropes with a piano accordion, all ivory and silver and red enamel, on his back. He bowed twice and played *Tiger Rag*, getting the tiger so well that lots of people threw pennies into the ring when he finished. Then he played a medley of songs like *My Old Dutch* and *Tipperary* and everyone sang, but when he stopped and got out a piece of wood, took his accordion off and started to tap-dance, the crowd started to boo. He had to play the accordion again, which was a shame, because Joe was interested in tap-dancing and liked to watch the arms and legs bent at the knees and the little head jerks.

A lot more pennies were thrown, then someone shouted, 'We want Python,' and a whole crowd took it up. Another crowd answered 'We want Hammer,' and soon you couldn't hear Sam playing at all. He stopped and looked down at the M.C.'s seat with a worried expression on his face. The M.C. came up and thanked Sam, who was picking up his pennies. He spread out a big poster on the floor and started to read out the programme for next week, but the noise was so great he gave up. He beckoned towards the door through which the other wrestlers had passed after their fight. A little wiry man in shirt sleeves and blue braces came bounding up the aisle, and leaped into the ring. After him marched the wrestlers.

First Shmule in a crimson dressing gown gleaming in the light, with Blackie and Oliver bustling round him. A man leaned over to pat his back as he passed, and when he sprang into the ring there was quite a big cheer. Shmule bowed towards the cheers and looked proudly at the small group who booed. He waved to Joe, and Joe waved back. Sonia blew kisses and Mr Kandinsky said, 'A fine boy, good luck to him.' Then Shmule started stretching himself, so as not to lose a moment's development.

After him came the dreaded Python with his manager, a man with a square blue jaw, like polished rock. The Python wore a black silk dressing gown and a white towel round his neck, and he towered above the seconds dancing round him. He climbed into the ring, not so full of spring as Shmule but with one powerful hitch of his arm. There was, true, a bigger cheer for Python, but Shmule's friends booed hard. Joe hissed like a goose, Sonia shouted out 'Carcase meat,' and Mr Kandinsky said 'What a bull.'

The M.C. introduced Shmule first. He called him the white hope of Aldgate, the sensational young former amateur championship contender, a clean-fighting local boy, and so on and so forth. All the while the Python was baring his teeth and growling and shaking his fist at Shmule's supporters. Shmule slipped out of his crimson dressing gown and now his muscles rippled in the ring lights, his spotless white hammer shining like a star against the crimson briefs. Oliver and Blackie clustered round his corner with towels and pails and a chair for him to sit on between rounds. They looked worried, although after all that saying he was a gonner, Shmule looked as if nothing could ever frighten him. There was a fresh feeling about him, as if he felt there were so many tailors expecting him to make a good fight, especially with the trade being so up and down, and so much unemployment, they lent him the strength they had been saving for work.

The dreaded Python Macklin was very angry. He strained like a fierce bulldog at the rope, just waiting for the bell to sound to throw himself on Shmule, tearing him limb from limb like the Christian martyrs, just as Mavis said. The black hair on the Python stood up in fury and he ground his teeth together. When the M.C. pointed in his direction and called out his name, famous contender for the championship of the world, and veteran of the ring all over Europe, the Python drew himself up and the muscles on his chest and back were swollen with pride and power. He grinned, his teeth clamped tight together, and when the red-haired woman screamed out, 'Murder him, Py,' he stared at her as if he was hungry and she was a juicy steak.

'A forty-minute contest,' the M.C. shouted through his megaphone, 'of eight five-minute rounds, for a purse of not ten, not twenty, but twenty-five pounds.'

He drew the two men together and whispered to them, the Python sneering, Shmule looking serious. Mr Kandinsky said again, 'Good luck,' and then the bell rang. In the sudden silence it echoed well.

Joe sat with his seat tipped up to see over the head of the man in front. This man had a head like a smooth water melon with a bit of hair round the edges, pasted down with oil as if painted. As soon as the bell rang he started to talk slowly in a gruff voice like a gate swinging on rusty hinges in the wind. The woman next to him had grey hair permanently waved and never spoke, except to say, 'Have a nut.' The man was very helpful to Joe because he was an expert and explained the whole fight, hold by hold.

At first the wrestlers circled watchfully round one another looking for an opening. The man with the painted head said, 'You watch, Em, he'll be on to him, just give him that opening, watch, it's coming – no, hold it, now – no, he missed it, he's waiting to put the scissors on him.'

The Python prepared to spring on Shmule, who stood quite still waiting. Then, as the Python bent his legs to jump, Shmule stepped aside and Python fell on his face with a heavy slap.

'He missed him,' said the man with painted hair, and even as he spoke Shmule leapt on to the Python, catching both legs below knee level in the crook of his arm, and pulling sharply.

'Ouch!' shouted Python.

'Ouff!' said the man with painted hair. 'He got the old calf-lock on him.'

The Python shook himself like an alligator, and one of his knees slipped free and bowled Shmule over. The Python caught hold of Shmule by the foot and thigh and prepared to throw him, but Shmule pressed into the canvas with both hands, and heaved his body into the Python's ribs like a battering ram. The Python reeled into the ropes, and the bell rang.

Shmule turned to his corner, but the Python came after him. The crowd roared with one voice, 'Look behind you!' Shmule turned sharply, and the referee jumped in front of Python, and forced him to his corner. The Python was furious and pushing his seconds off the ring, he picked up his chair and punched his fist through the seat.

'Phoo,' said the man with painted hair, 'what a round, the dirty bastard turning on him like that after the bell, the dirty great bleeder.'

'Have some nuts, Fred,' the permanently waved woman said.

'The swine,' said Sonia with tears in her eyes, 'did you see that?'

The seconds rubbed them down and waved towels while the wrestlers spat into pails, and breathed deep and even, glaring at one another across the ring, listening to their manager's advice. The crowd wasn't shouting, 'Carve up,' any more. They could see it was serious. The bell rang for the second round.

The Python at once shot from his corner, his fingers crooked to seize Shmule, his face rigid, calling the muscles of his body to attention. Shmule crouched like a panther, waiting.

'He's giving him half a stone,' the man with the painted head said. 'He's got to play a waiting game, let the Python use hisself up, then come in quick. Ahh!'

The Python had his arms about Shmule and was hugging him like a bear. Shmule's arms were pinned to his sides, and he couldn't move. He twisted to one side then to the other, but the Python shortened the hug, working the grip of one hand upon the other wrist slowly up his arm. Shmule's face twisted with pain.

'Let him get out of that one,' the man said. Sonia clenched and unclenched her hands, and Joe's mother looked away. Mr Kandinsky was breathing hard, but Joe just stared, wondering what Shmule would do now. The crowd was shouting, 'Finish him, Python!'

Then Shmule moved his hand up and down in fast little movements against his thigh, and the referee jumping about watching saw the sign, and told Python to let go, the Hammer gave in. But Python wouldn't let go, and Shmule bit his lips in agony. Now the crowd shouted against the Python but that didn't help Shmule. The referee and all the seconds jumped on to him to tear him away, and the bell rang.

Blackie and Oliver helped Shmule to his corner and gently rubbed him, putting wet towels on his face. The crowd was furious with the Python, but he didn't care. He shouted back at them, showing off his muscles and asking if any one would like to try them. 'Filth!' Mr Kandinsky shouted, but poor Shmule looked pale and his eyes were closed.

'He's a dirty fighter,' the man with painted hair said, 'but give credit, he's got a grip like iron, the bleeder.'

'Get us some more nuts, Fred,' the woman replied.

Blackie and Oliver were working hard on Shmule, who breathed deeply, the colour coming back into his face. By the time the bell rang for the third round, he seemed as good as new.

'But you can't tell,' the man with the painted head said, 'he could have a couple ribs broke clean and he wouldn't know till after.'

'Has he got a couple ribs broke?' Joe asked.

'God forbid,' Mr Kandinsky answered, 'God forbid.'

Blackie and Oliver must have told Shmule not to waste time, because he came out fast and made straight for the Python, who being pleased with himself, was a bit careless. Shmule clasped his hands together and raised them for a rabbit punch, but he was too late. The Python crouched away, out of distance, not careless any more. Then a look of pain suddenly crossed Shmule's face, and the Python grinned and came in to attack, his hands low.

'He's hurt,' Sonia whispered.

'He's hurt all right,' the man in front of Joe said.

But what a surprise. Shmule suddenly leaped forward and caught the Python a great crack on the jaw with his left fist. The Python looked surprised and fell down.

'No boxing,' the crowd yelled.

The Python started to get up at once, but Shmule was on top of him, his knees to either side of his stomach, his hands firmly planted on his shoulders, pressing them to the canvas. As he pressed he strengthened the grip of his knees. The Python groaned, shouted. He jerked and jumped and twisted, but he couldn't throw Shmule off.

'He can give it,' the man said, 'but he can't take it. Go on, boy, do him!'

The Python beat the floor with both hands and Shmule let go at once.

'Good boy,' the man said.

'He should give him the same as he got,' Sonia said, 'why should he fight him clean.'

The crowd cheered Shmule, but the Python wasn't hurt as much as they thought, because as soon as Shmule broke away, he leapt to his feet. Not fast enough though. Shmule wasn't so green now. He didn't stop watching the Python for a second, and he saw him tensed to leap. Ready for him, he caught the Python another crack on the chin as he came up. The Python went down with Shmule on top of him, but he was saved by the bell.

'That's more like it,' the man said, 'he's got the old Python on the squirm, proper.'

'Get us some nuts, Fred,' the woman said.

'Fancy an ice?' the man asked.

'Some nuts, Fred,' the woman said again.

'How's the boy doing now, Sonia?' Mr Kandinsky asked.

'He's all right,' Sonia said, 'another round like that and he'll win.'

'We're winning,' Joe told his mother.

'That's good,' she replied. 'It's awful to see their faces.'

In the fourth round the Python set out to finish Shmule off. He tried all the fancy holds, the Indian death lock, the flying mare, the cobra, but Shmule was like an eel, he didn't stay still long enough for the grips to take.

'He's using his speed now,' the man said, 'let's see the Python catch up with that.'

But the Python couldn't catch up with that. After a couple of minutes the crowd started to laugh, because the Python lumbered like a great ox, while Shmule danced circles round him, cracking him on the back and chest every so often. Now the Python was on his guard against face blows, and being careful made him ever more clumsy. He was furious with the crowd for laughing. He looked at Shmule through slit eyes wanting to murder him.   .

'Let me get my hands on you, laughing boy, that's all,' he growled.

Then suddenly Shmule nipped in close, his foot jabbed out, and the Python fell heavily on to the canvas, his arms round Shmule's leg. But as he fell Shmule struck the Python a heavy blow to the stomach, and pulled his leg free.

The Python held on to his stomach with both hands. His head came forward. His neck bent towards Shmule like a beast to the slaughterer.

Shmule folded his hands together as if to pray. He lifted them and carefully aiming, brought a rabbit punch with all his force clean on to the Python's neck. The Python slumped forward over his hands. Shmule stood back, watching. The Python didn't move.

'Cold meat!' someone shouted.

'Hammer!' all the tailors yelled.

'Hammer!' shouted Joe.

The Python was out cold.

ELEVEN

IT was the latest night ever. It was late when Joe and his mother and Mr Kandinsky left Sonia at the swimming baths waiting for Shmule, both of them to follow on later. It was late when they got home, but no one suggested that Joe should go to bed, because it was, after all, an occasion. Joe said it was only fair to bring Africana in since he had been such a help, but Mr Kandinsky said, 'Leave him sleep. Tomorrow is also a day.'

Joe's mother lit the gas fire in the kitchen, and put the kettle on the stove to make a cup of tea. As they waited for the kettle Mr Kandinsky told them about the patent steam presser which, only four years old, he could buy for practically nothing from the Grosvenor Garment Company in Fournier Street. With a bit of patching up, tighten a few screws, a good re-padding job, scrape off the rust, a coat of paint, it would make a first-class presser, good as new.

Now Mr Kandinsky didn't have Shmule to worry about any more, he could concentrate on the steam presser again. In fact, now that Shmule had actually won the fight, it seemed unreasonable to Mr Kandinsky that he shouldn't have the presser.

'A chance like this, Becky,' he said, 'doesn't, after all, come up every day. A chance of a lifetime. He would take thirty pound for it he said, but I know better. He would be glad to get twenty pound as well. After all, all the big firms can buy new pressers, what do they want with an old machine four years old, rusty, dirty? And whose got thirty pounds who isn't a big firm? Believe me, he would be glad to take twenty. And yet whose got even twenty?'

'Shmule has got twenty-five pounds because you heard, the winner gets twenty-five pounds to himself,' Joe said.

Mr Kandinsky looked thunderstruck. He slapped his forehead with his palm. 'You're right, Joe,' he said. 'Shmule has got twenty-five pounds.'

Joe's mother looked over from the stove where she was pouring boiling water into the teapot.

'Shmule must buy Sonia a ring before anything else,' she said. 'It's a shame otherwise.'

'That's true,' Mr Kandinsky said, pursing his lips. 'Quite right. Mind you, if Shmule was to come along to me and tell me, I bought the steam presser, what about a partnership, I would tell him straightaway, certainly. But naturally Sonia must have a ring. Only this other way she wouldn't just be a girl with a ring marrying a young fellow, a worker in the tailoring. This way she is marrying a guvnor, a partner in a business, and what is more, a growing business. Because I tell you, Becky, with a patent steam presser we can take in so much jobbing, we can make a living from this alone. Still, Sonia must have a ring. Maybe it is the only chance Shmule gets his whole life, but doesn't matter. A ring is important.'

Mr Kandinsky was very upset. It was selfish of Sonia to stop Shmule becoming a guvnor. Mr Kandinsky pressed the lemon in his glass with a spoon. Joe sipped his milk, wondering what Africana would do about this. Then they heard voices on the stairs.

Shmule and Sonia came in arm in arm. Though he looked tired, Shmule's eye were bright.

'I couldn't get him away from there,' Sonia said. 'They all wanted to see him.'

Mr Kandinsky gripped Shmule's hand.

'Good luck to you always,' he said, 'good health, and every blessing.'

Joe's mother said, 'It was awful to watch, but you were marvellous, Shmule, marvellous. Only don't let him do it any more, Sonia. You mustn't do it any more, Shmule. Buy Sonia a ring now, and finish with the wrestling.'

'She's right,' Mr Kandinsky said. 'It's for the beast of the field.'

'You know what he told me round one?' Shmule said. 'He told me to lie down in the seventh, I could share the purse with him. That's what he told me.'

'That Python,' Sonia said, angry, 'he wanted Shmule to lie down.'

'When I tell him I am fighting clean he says he'll ruin me.'

'You hear,' Mr Kandinsky said to all of them. 'You hear what kind of a business this wrestling is?'

'It kills you for real development of the body beautiful,' Sonia said.

'No good for the muscular tone or the efficiency,' Shmule said. 'Still, I can give baby a ring.'

Sonia hugged him.

'I want to talk to you with a serious proposition,' Mr Kandinsky said, clearing his throat and holding his hand up for silence. 'Namely, now that you got a bit of capital, and I am, after all, the truth is the truth, an old man. Namely a partnership deal.'

Shmule looked more dazed than the dreaded Python the last time he was hit. Sonia hugged him again.

'Baby,' she said, 'you hear?'

'But,' continued Mr Kandinsky, and he explained that Shmule would have to bring with him a patent steam presser.

'Thank you very much,' said Shmule, 'for a hundred eighty-seven pounds a patent presser. Not two?'

'Don't grab,' Mr Kandinsky said, 'listen a minute.' He told him about the second-hand presser over at Grosvenor Garments.

'You think he would take twenty?' Shmule asked, stroking his lip.

'Take?' answered Mr Kandinsky. 'He would drag it out of your hands.'

Sonia didn't say anything. Her face couldn't make up its mind whether she was pleased or not. It was a difficult decision.

'Let me speak to Sonia a minute,' Mr Kandinsky said. 'Sonia,' he said, 'here you are a young woman in the bloom of her beauty, a perfect mate for life with this Maccabeus here.'

Sonia blushed and looked at Shmule.

'Two years you have been patient,' Mr Kandinsky continued. 'Listen, Sonia, this is important. Two years you have lived on the word of this man alone. No ring to bind the promise, so that sometimes other people, busybodies with big mouths, who didn't know what kind of girl you are, they said, "Look at Sonia, no ring. What kind of an engagement?" ' Mr Kandinsky paused.

Sonia's eyes were full of tears as she listened. It was no more than the truth. She had been marvellous, it was true.

Mr Kandinsky continued. 'Sonia,' he said, 'they didn't know this boy, what a fighter he is, how clean and honest, and what a worker, no one to touch him in the entire East End. Him they saw tonight. Now they know what he is. And you saw him, too, what he will do for you, to get you a better ring than any girl in Novak Blouses ever had.'

'Gay-day Blouses,' Sonia said tenderly.

'Gay-day,' Mr Kandinsky repeated. 'But something else no girl in Gay-day ever had. You know what it is?' He pointed to Sonia to answer the question. She shook her head.

'They didn't marry a fellow who was, already, so young, a guvnor in his own business. That's what they didn't have.'

Mr Kandinsky made his last point in a loud voice, his pointing finger sweeping round the whole world to find another girl who could say she had done better than Sonia.

'Now, Sonia,' he continued after a moment in which Sonia squeezed Shmule's hand. 'I ask you straight out. Which is better, such a husband, a champion, a guvnor, with the world in front of him. Or a fiancé, works for Kandinsky, the Fashion Street trousers-maker, wrestles Saturday night to make a few pound, he might be able to get married one day to a girl at Gay-day Blouses with a big diamond ring? Don't answer me,' he went on as Sonia opened her mouth. 'Think first. It is in your hands, his life, your life, I don't want to influence you. Drink a cup of tea and think.'

That was how Mr Kandinsky made Shmule his partner, and though everyone was pleased, they said Joe should be in bed.

TWELVE

THE next morning was fine and sunny. When Joe woke up he heard the horses clopping over the cobbles, and goods trains rattling from the arches. The first thing he thought was he must tell Africana. He dressed quietly, and leaving his mother to have her Sunday morning lie-in, ran downstairs.

Mr Kandinsky was already at work, and Joe shouted good morning and rushed into the yard.

'Good old unicorn,' he shouted out to Africana, but there was no rustle from Africana's house. The house looked like a pile of old boxes waiting to be chopped up for firewood, desolate. Africana was gone.

'He's gone,' Joe shouted, running back to the workroom, 'He's gone, Mr Kandinsky, he's gone.'

'What?' said Mr Kandinsky. 'Whose gone?'

'Africana's gone, he's just gone,' Joe cried, and how would he ever bring his father back from Africa?

'Let's have a look,' Mr Kandinsky said. 'Let's keep our head and look.'

They searched the yard carefully.

'Let's look in the house again,' Mr Kandinsky said.

'It's empty,' Joe replied, tears coming fast. 'Can't you see, it's empty.'

'Let's look all the same,' said Mr Kandinsky.

He searched through the bed of remnants.

'What's this?' he said. He bent down and picked up something It was a gleaming golden sovereign. He handed it to Joe.

'What is it?' asked Joe.

'Come inside, Joe,' Mr Kandinsky said. 'I will tell you.'

'He's gone,' Joe said, the tears still there.

'Come inside,' said Mr Kandinsky, and he put his arm round Joe's shoulder.

'You know what this is, Joe?' he asked, giving him the sovereign. 'This is a golden sovereign. And what has happened is plain as my nose. You could see yourself that unicorn didn't do so well in Fashion Street, ailing the whole time, no interest, miserable the whole day. So you know what he's done? He's gone back to Africa like you said he should. But just to show it's nothing personal, he left this golden sovereign on account of that magic horn worth five thousand pound.'

'Ten thousand,' said Joe.

'Ten thousand pound I mean,' continued Mr Kandinsky. 'Meanwhile, keep this for luck.'

'He won't come back,' Joe said.

'Maybe not,' Mr Kandinsky replied. 'Unicorns can't grow in Fashion Street, but boys have to.'

Joe went upstairs slowly, rubbing the golden sovereign between his fingers. There was a small rough piece broken on top of it but otherwise it was like the coin on Mr Kandinsky's father's watch chain, which made two golden sovereigns in the house.

When his mother came into the kitchen, her face blanched with sleep, Joe asked whether two sovereigns would bring his father back. It was the only thing the unicorn had forgotten to arrange. With the sleep still on her, she didn't know at first what he meant. After Joe explained carefully, she said yes, it was a great help, and they would find his father's return passage money somehow. They would never go to Africa, it was a dream, but he would come back to them, he would come back soon. Next week she must see about Joe starting school. He was growing up learning nothing about life.

Joe rolled the sovereign on the table thinking that if all the pets he had ever had were in the yard now, he could charge people pennies to come in. They would cheer and throw more pennies when they saw Africana's shining horn stretching high above the slate rooftops.

After breakfast he went into the yard to play, although he had no special game in mind. For a little while he missed Africana but soon he thought of something. In the end, it brought him safely to Africa.